CW00616837

HE DIED WITH HIS BOOTS OFF

Fresh out of prison, Bob Oak expected little good of anybody or anything, and it seemed well in keeping with his luck when he arrived at his uncle's home in Coopville and found George Oak lying newly dead upon the floor. It was curious that the murdered man should have died with his boots so conspicuously removed, but Bob had little time for the talk of a treasure map that had supposedly been hidden in the boots – until Heidi Schirmer actually handed the scrap of vellum to him.

The finding of the treasure map lead to much death and duplicity. But would it lead Oak to the notorious Aztec treasure?

He Died With His Boots Off

DAN ROYAL

A Black Horse Western

ROBERT HALE · LONDON

© Dan Royal 1991
First published in Great Britain 1991

ISBN 0 7090 4477 1

Robert Hale Limited
Clerkenwell House
Clerkenwell Green
London EC1R 0HT

Photoset in North Wales by
Derek Doyle & Associates, Mold, Clwyd.
Printed in Great Britain by
St Edmundsbury Press, Bury St Edmunds, Suffolk.
Bound by WBC Bookbinders Ltd, Bridgend, Glamorgan.

One

Bob Oak looked up the garden path towards his Uncle George's house. The place had about the same appearance as ever. It was foul of window, short a tile or two, and lacking a coat of paint. But such domestic trivia had never bothered George Oak all that much. If you had dealings with him of any kind, you simply had to accept that he had been committed to sloth, whisky, and foolish women for the last thirty years and wasn't likely to change his ways for anybody. George Oak had slid through life, around the law, and would eventually make it past St Peter in the same fashion. But, with all his faults, he wasn't the worst of men by a long chalk, and that was why his nephew – who wasn't perfect either – had accepted Uncle George's written invitation to visit him. That and, of course, the photograph that his uncle had promised him of his late mother.

Casting a quick glance to where he had recently tied his horse at the picket fence, Oak opened the gate before him and walked along the garden path towards the front door of the dwelling. Reaching it, he knocked and, hearing movement in the living room beyond, prepared to lift the latch and enter – as had been his custom through his boyhood and teens – but, to his mild surprise, he felt the woodwork jar strongly against the knuckles of his right hand and heard the key grate in the lock. 'Uncle George!' he called. 'It's me – Bob!'

Slightly muffled, an explosion thudded, splinters of wood flew from the door, and a bullet whipped the slack of Oak's leather waistcoat. Badly startled now, he backed off as the revolver indoors boomed again and a second bullet smashed through the woodwork opposite him, once more narrowly missing his body. It was too much; he threw himself upon his face, sure that the gun in the house had not finished banging yet, and three more shots boomed at him, the slugs tearing through the already ruined door and reducing its middle planking to a pepper pot of ragged holes out of which threads of blue gunsmoke twisted.

Oak lay there gasping. He was unhurt, but figured that he had been scared out of a year's growth, and a few moments went by before he recovered to the extent that he was able to rise to his left knee and bellow: 'Have you gone crazy, George Oak? Do you want to kill your nephew? What's up with you, man?'

There was no reply, but Oak was sure that he heard hasty movements, heavy and clumsy, at the further end of the house, which stood veiled by the hanging foliage of birch, ash, and wild apple trees, and gave onto a slope that was similarly wooded all the way up to the ridge that sheltered both the dwelling itself and the nearby town of Coopville – where Bob Oak had first seen the light of day and grown to manhood – from the north wind.

Oak straightened up. He was still greatly annoyed. It sounded as if Uncle George had taken flight. The fellow had gone loco sure enough. Either that or he was blind drunk again and suffering from the d.t.'s. Lifting a foot, Oak was tempted to kick the door in, but he checked his violent impulse just in time – realizing that enough damage had already been done and that the terms of his parole required that he moderate his behaviour – and walked off to his left and rounded the front corner of the house on that side, taking deep breaths all the time to quell his fiery emotions.

He came to a window, his right arm almost brushing the sill and, without really meaning to check, peered in through the dusty glass. He expected to see no more than a furnished room beyond, but promptly received another frightful shock; for he saw Uncle George lying flat upon his back near the sideboard. A pool of blood covered the floor about George Oak's head, and his face wore the empty expression that only death could bring.

Filled abruptly with galvanic force, Bob Oak sprang round and raced back to the front door. Here he lifted a boot again, and this time drove it against the woodwork with all his power. He expected the door to burst open at once, but it merely shuddered, and he got a not better result when he repeated the battery. Realizing now that the lock was far stronger than he had expected, he lowered his left shoulder and put it to work in place of his foot, getting the whole of his two hundred and twenty pounds behind it; but the door still resisted him and, cursing, he redoubled his efforts, one charge succeeding the next, until the door finally flew open and went whirling round on its hinges, crashing to rest against the inner wall on his right.

Gasping from his efforts, Oak stumbled into the living room and, massaging a bruise or two, sank onto his knees beside the man lying there. One glance was enough to assure him that he had seen nothing from the window that was not truly there. Uncle George was unquestionably dead. The back of his skull had been smashed in, and blood was still streaming from the wound to form a rapidly expanding pool. The older man had been struck down within the last few minutes – and the heavy iron poker that had been used to accomplish the deed was lying on the floor beside his right elbow. On the evidence, Bob Oak had actually surprised the killer in his crime, and that explained the sudden locking of the door, the murderous gunshots that had followed it, and the noises of flight in which the incident had ended.

Oak pushed himself erect again. He gazed towards the lower end of the room. There were two doors in the wall there; and one on the right and the other on the left. That on the right – which served the passage that gave access to the two bedrooms – gaped wide, and he could see down the length of the corridor beyond to the dwelling's northern wall, where an open window appeared to indicate the killer's escape route.

Feeling the inner pressure to do it – though the action seemed pointless now that so much time had elapsed – Bob Oak ran out of the living room and into the corridor that crossed the bedroom doors, his steps speeding as he headed down the narrow space, and he almost literally jumped through the casement and landed calf-deep in the grass outside.

There he paused, his vision obscured by the foliage of the trees about him, and looked high, seeking any trace of the man who had gone before him on the steep slope that was sufficiently visible ahead. But the birch and aspens above yielded nothing, and he lowered his gaze to the grass at his feet, perceiving faint tracks in the growth that pointed the next stage of the murderer's escape path. Now Oak resumed what he felt could be described only dubiously as the pursuit and traversed the ground between the back wall of the house and the slope which sheltered it.

Reaching the foot of the grade, he started to climb, his huge frame no asset in this situation, and he toiled upwards through the bushes and trees that were quite densely present – moving at once too fast and with too little concentration to

spot further traces of his quarry underfoot or
amidst the growth above the ground – and he
topped out a minute or two later and turned his
sweating face to the breeze, drawing down all the
extra air that he needed to restore his panting
lungs to normal.

As the discomfort in his chest grew less, Oak set
his arms akimbo and looked northwards over the
sprawling green of the forests in that quarter,
lifting his eyes to the pastel splendours of the San
Juan mountains about half a world away; but the
space and beauty of the north held very little
significance for him just then, since he could not
believe that the killer had actually crossed the
ridge and descended into the country out there.

Listening to the intimations of his subcon-
scious, Oak felt reasonably sure that his Uncle
George's killer had been somebody not unknown
to the older man: a townsman probably; and one
who, if he had come this high – and there was no
real certainty that he had – would have turned
right and followed the summit along, with the
intention of descending into Coopville itself from a
position perhaps a quarter of a mile to the east of
the present spot.

Oak started wandering townwards along the
crest, his movements gradually losing all sense of
purpose, and he was beginning to ask himself
what the dickens he was doing up here – and how
the devil he was going to handle the difficult
situation that he found himself in when he got
down again – when something fragmentary, and

of a man-made colouration, drew his eyes to the gap between two patches of blackthorn a short distance ahead.

The aimlessness left Oak's movements. He crossed quickly to the tussocks between the parallel clumps of bush. Here he picked up about three square inches of the type of cork filling used by shoemakers to cushion the space between a boot's inner and outer soles. He turned the piece of waxed cork over and over in his fingers, wondering how it had got up here – for it was undoubtedly fresh to the air – but, though the mystery of its presence was intriguing, it was hardly a find to get excited about for itself.

He strolled clear of the bushes, frowning to himself as he remembered something about his uncle's body that had seemed unimportant before. George Oak had been lying there in his stockinged feet. Well, a man in his own house could certainly go shoe or slipperless if he wished, and Uncle George, as previously acknowledged, had not been particular in any aspect of his domestic life. The find up here could just possibly have some significance after all. It might be worth looking around further.

A small movement, way ahead and low, plucked at the corner of Oak's right eye. Moving to the southern edge of the crest, he looked forward and down. Possessed of excellent vision, he made out a figure – perhaps four hundred yards beyond him – passing off the base of the ridge and into the lots along Coopville's northern edge. Though hunched

of shoulder and hurried of stride, the man
appeared a tall one and was dressed – so far as
Oak could be sure – in a grey shirt and a pair of
sand-coloured trousers. Beyond those details, Oak
could discern nothing, and the other soon
vanished among the buildings at the back of town
and did not reappear again at any spot that the
watcher's eye could reach.

Oak gave his gunbelt a little hitch. Had he just
glimpsed his uncle's killer? The man had certainly
emerged from the background at about the right
place and time. But that, of course, was far from
conclusive. The man might have been doing
almost anything on the ridge, and simply been in
the wrong place at the right time from the
standpoint of his, Oak's, observations. Nor,
though he was familiar with the people of
Coopville, did he have the faintest idea of the
other's identity; so, all things considered, he
would probably be wise to forget about what he
had just seen for the time being.

He began to cast around him again, half
convinced on the evidence of the piece of cork that
there was more to find up here as yet and, as he
strayed across the summit and approached the
northern edge again, he came upon the much-
severed remains of a leather bootlace that had
obviously been parted in a succession of places by
the blade of a knife which had been inserted at top
or bottom of the parallel lines of eyelets and
slashed up or down between them in one go.

This seemed to be further evidence of the

violence done to a boot, and it quickened Oak's interest and kept him searching, until the discovery of a further piece of cork, right on the northern brink itself, caused him to look over and down. His gaze, concentrated now, roved across the bushes and tussocks below, and very soon he saw, trapped against the dead growth along the base of a thicket, what was left of not one boot but a pair that had been cast down from up here in a dismembered state and come to rest where he saw them now.

Reversing himself, since the grade beneath him was steep enough to be approached with care, Oak began to descend the northern face of the ridge. Meeting with no real difficulties as he climbed down, he soon came to where the boots – or what remained of them – lay. He picked one up, holding it with care, for it was baggy of upper, bearded of frayed stitching, and otherwise falling apart at the slightest pressure. Looking around the ruin, he deduced that its wanton destruction had been brought about by the cutting of the stitching which had joined upper and welt. The separation at this point, from heel to toe and back again down the opposite side, had simply caused the boot to drop in halves and exposed all the hidden work which had gone into making it strong and comfortable. Indeed, the boot had no secrets left, and that made Oak wonder anew.

Dropping the bits and pieces of the first, he went to the second boot and, picking it up, saw that it had been destroyed in a manner similar to its twin. The damage was deliberate, calculated, and total and, as in the previous case, had served no discernible end except to turn the article of footwear inside out. Short of a childish malice being present, Oak could only conclude that the boots had been cut apart to facilitate a search of their interior or to see how they had been made. But the latter possibility had no real place in his credence, since the obvious haste that was visible in the cutting strongly suggested that the user of the knife had been a disturbed man under pressure. Perhaps one who had recently committed murder and had some fear of being pursued.

Thinking in terms of evidence, Oak bundled together the remains of the pair of boots and, holding them in his left hand, climbed back gingerly up the northern face of the ridge, making it with the odd slip but soon standing safely again in the cooler air that blew across the crest. Then, not perceiving anything else of use that he could do on the summit, he returned to the head of his ascent from the late George Oak's home and started down again, reaching the bottom shortly afterwards and then walking round to the front of the house.

Entering at the bullet-shattered door, he saw the body lying sprawled before him just as he had left it, though the bleeding from the head wound had now stopped and the red pool in which the base of the skull rested was beginning to congeal. Conscious of flies buzzing around – no doubt attracted by the presence of blood and imminent decay – Oak walked wide of the corpse and placed the dismembered boots on the dining table adjacent.

Feeling suddenly drained and baffled, he pulled a chair from beneath the table and sat down, avoiding the dead face on the floor and asking himself in what degree George Oak could have been to blame for his own fate, since he had invariably been mixed up in activities best left alone and kept some pretty low company because of it.

True, the George Oak of more recent years had not been the wild man of half a lifetime ago, and his nephew could now be judging him too harshly; but the extreme violence of his death did hint at the hand of an enraged enemy. Whatever the exact truth of that, however, there was obviously a story that had culminated here. The whole business needed professional investigation. Though increasingly uneasy of the need, he had better get along to the sheriff's office without delay. His position was clearly a delicate one, and he did not wish to antagonise the law. Sneed Buckley was no Pinkerton ace, but he wore the badge in Coopville; and, even if Bob Oak had neither faith in his work nor liking for the man himself, Buckley was the fellow whom he must approach to obtain help and a hearing.

Getting to his feet again, Oak pushed the chair back under the table and headed for the door. He supposed he had better lock the house up, and put the key in his pocket until he could hand it to the sheriff; and he was about to begin doing what he had envisaged, when he remembered the open window at the further end of the house.

Turning, he walked into the passage that served the bedrooms, his steps becoming more uncertain all the time, and he was only a pace or two short of the casement when it occurred to him that the window had presumably been opened by the killer and that this represented evidence of a sort. Anyway, he had better leave the damned thing alone; and he turned again, shaking his head over the woolly thinking that had created the need, and had started retracing his steps, when he became aware that two men had entered the front door while he was through here and were standing just short of the dead man in the living room.

His apprehension on the increase, Oak kept walking forward, and the older of the pair – a thick-set man of slightly more than middle height, who wore the sheriff's star upon his chest – eyed him suspiciously and then drew his revolver. 'To me,' he ordered, 'and quick about it!'

'Look here, Sneed –' Oak began.

'Shut up!' the sheriff interrupted. 'That damned tongue of yours was always too ready, Bob Oak. Well, it looks to me as if you're in the kind of trouble now you'll never be able to talk your way out of. I didn't like your uncle, but I never guessed we'd one day have to hang his nephew for his murder.'

Oak couldn't credit it. Everything had again come out amiss. He had realized that his situation was a delicate one, but he had never dreamed that it could be interpreted like this.

Two

A sense of fear and outrage grew in Bob Oak. He felt that he was being judged out of hand. Although he had been told to shut up, he knew that an immediate protest was vital; since, once false beliefs had settled, men were likely to go on responding to them beyond contrary argument and accepting them as unalterable truth. Stubborn men mostly made their own right, and Oak knew Sneed Buckley for a stubborn man. 'Sheriff,' he said hotly, 'you don't know anything about me right now. You start taking a few facts to check. I've just ridden down from Colorado. I hadn't seen my uncle in six years. I came because he invited me by letter. I know as little about –'

'Sure,' the sheriff cut in again, 'those are facts I can check, but how do they relate to what's here? What else are you trying to say?'

'I was starting to tell you when you stopped me,' Oak said shortly. 'I know as little about George Oak's recent life as I say you know about mine. I've had no contact with him for six years. If you don't know anything about a man's affairs, what

18

reason can you have to kill him?'

'How did that sound to you, Tod?' Sheriff
Buckley asked his deputy, a lean, lantern-jawed
young man, opaque of eye, very sharp of nose, and
ill-connected at the joints.

'Weak,' came the response.

'Like your head, Landers,' Oak said rudely. 'We
sat side by side in school, and you were too dense
to know morning from night. How the devil did
you ever get to be a lawman?'

'Not as easily as you got to be a lowdown killer!'
Tod Landers snorted in response. 'Some of us ain't
as fast as others. I had to make up for lost time.'

'From Plymouth Rock, maybe?' Oak shot back,
inwardly dismayed at his own recklessness, for
that damned parole hung like a sword above his
head – and here he was spitting at the very people
who could hurt him most. Yet he felt that, in the
present company, he had to defend himself as
strongly as he knew how. 'I'll thank you not to call
me a killer, Landers. That I am not. It's fine for
you to hide behind a tin star.'

'You are out of your mind, Bob Oak!' Sneed
Buckley declared, the pop-eyed expression on his
face bespeaking an amazement too deep to come
up with anything more original. 'Do you imagine
you can say whatever you please and we're going
to listen?'

'I walked up to that door, Sheriff,' Oak retorted,
ignoring the question-mark. 'I knocked on it,
heard movement in here, called my uncle's name,
then got shot at through the woodwork. Look for

yourself! How much evidence do you need?' He
gave Buckley a moment in which to look round.
'Hell – next I had a peep in through the window. I
saw Uncle George lying there. After that I busted
my way into the house; and then I chased off up to
the ridge, hoping to sight the killer – and, while I
was up there, I found that pair of boots you see
lying cut up on the table.'

'You didn't cut them up like that?' the sheriff
queried.

'I did not.'

'Are they your uncle's boots?' Buckley asked.

'Well, he's not wearing any, Sneed, and any fool
can see that knife job is mighty recent.'

'A fact is what's sure,' Buckley commented, 'but
you want me to accept what's likely as one. I can't
be certain those boots were your uncle's. I can't be
sure about anything you've said. You always were
a rare liar. You were known for it around the
town.'

'I am not a liar, Sheriff.'

'You are too!' Tod Landers protested. 'You was
always telling whoppers. The stories you stuck
into me!'

'Stories, yes,' Oak admitted, grinning despite
himself. 'You'd believe any old fairytale, Tod!'

'So you are a liar – and a killer!'

'Get that look off your face, Oak!' the sheriff
rapped out. 'You are a killer. Let there be no
mistake about that. You were tried and convicted,
and you've just done six years in the Denver
penitentiary as proof of it.'

'It was not a killing,' Oak said quietly. 'It was self-defence. That tinhorn was about to try it on with a sneak pistol. I had no choice but to shoot him.'

'There was no doubt,' Buckley conceded. 'Personally, I had no belief in it. But it saved your neck. They were cracking down mighty hard on gunplay at that time. They'd have hanged you high if it hadn't been they found that derringer on Jack Royal.'

'He was too slow to get it into the open,' Oak said.

'Or was it you were a shade too fast to let him?' the sheriff inquired cynically.

'If your life's threatened,' Oak flung back, 'you shoot and get it over with. You've as much cause to know that as I have, Sneed. You've never been afraid to face fire, and neither have I. Some wrong I've done, no doubt; but I've never been a coward. That should be further proof I'd never strike an old man down from behind.'

'You're too glib in your own defence,' Buckley said contemptuously. 'Six years is a long time, and prison changes a man. Maybe the Colorado jail turned you into a coward. Perhaps you had easy pickings in mind when you rode up to that fence out yonder. There's no quieter way of killing a man than by smashing his head in with a poker.'

'He was my uncle, g'dammit!'

'So what? How much money have you got in your pocket?'

'Ten dollars.'

'That won't take you far, will it?'

'Your mind's an ugly place, Sneed,' Oak remarked. 'What brought you to this house? Wasn't it the noise of gunshots – reported, or actually heard by you or Tod?'

'Never mind about what brought us here.'

'But I do mind,' Oak gritted. 'You're trying to cobble up a case against me, and pokers and gunshots hardly go together in one man's doings. Not in the same minute, they don't.'

'So who killed your uncle if you didn't?'

'The fellow who cut up that boot,' Oak answered bitterly. 'I can't put a name to him, but he may be wearing a grey shirt and sandy trousers.'

'Pete Br –,' Tod Landers began; but his boss cut him short with a negative so violently uttered that it made even Oak jump.

'When I want to hear from you again, Tod,' Buckley added, 'I'll let you know.'

'Sorry,' Landers pouted. 'But it sure sounded like he was speaking of –'

'Pete Brett?' Oak asked narrowly, naming his worst enemy in town from the old days.

'Don't jump to conclusions,' the sheriff advised.

'What's been done here is his kind of wickedness.'

'You heard me.'

Oak gazed down at Buckley, his face growing harder by the moment. 'It was Pete Brett who alerted you, Sneed, and you're protecting the varmint for some reason.'

'I shan't tell you again!'

'There's too much talk here, and not enough do.'

'There'll be do soon enough,' Sneed Buckley promised ominously. 'You say your uncle invited you here by letter.'

'By a letter I received close to the day they let me out,' Oak agreed. 'Figures word of my parole was published down here in New Mexico by the newspapers.'

'That's right,' the sheriff said curtly. 'Have you still got that letter?'

'Right here – on me.'

'Let's see it.'

Oak dug into his right-hand trouser-pocket. He took from it the now dirty page of a tradesman's account book that had been folded in four. 'There you are,' he said, passing it to Sneed Buckley.

Buckley unfolded the page. 'I see,' he said, wrinkling his nostrils as he deciphered the words that a sprawling, childish hand had inscribed in powdery black ink across the three-coloured ruling on the paper. 'I'm going to read it out. "Dear Neffy, I hear they're soon going to free you. I reckon you're counting off the days. Prison's no place for a man. Specially not for one of the Oak tribe.

"Howsomever, I reckon it's all in a lifetime, and you will have accepted it as such. Me and Coopville are still here. So why don't you ride down this way and give your old uncle a look? I've got that photograph of your ma you asked for. I've had it silver-framed, and you can have it when I see you. I know you thought a lot of your ma, as did I, and I reckon she's been piping her eye up in heaven over what they done to you.

"You're going to need a new life, Bob, and I'm not going to suggest you stick around Coopville. I haven't heard of paying work around here for years. No harm us talking about it all the same. I'm sure I'll be able to put you onto something you'll like some place. Your loving uncle, et cetera".' Buckley pulled a face. 'So that's it, Oak. Well, it proves you had the invitation to come here, but it doesn't prove you didn't kill your uncle.'

'How could it?' Oak demanded. 'But do you go and murder somebody who's got your well-being at heart?'

'Aw, George Oak promised much,' the sheriff observed disdainfully, 'but delivered little.'

That, unhappily, was true; but Bob Oak was not going to admit it.

'Where's the photograph?' Buckley asked.

'It used to be kept in the sideboard,' Oak replied.

Buckley pointed to the piece of furniture. 'Look in there and see, Tod.'

The deputy moved to the sideboard. Crouching, he opened the twin doors that formed the lower part of its front. Oak gazed over Landers' left shoulder. There was nothing within the space revealed; only empty shelves and the odd cobweb were on view. So, rising, the deputy pulled out the top drawers, striking lucky in that on the right, where the photograph of a stern-featured but distinctly handsome woman lay on a bolt of gingham. 'I reckon this is it,' Landers said, lifting the likeness and handing it to the sheriff.

'Your mama?' Buckley asked, showing the photograph to Oak.

Oak nodded. 'She's been dead these twelve years. Never did get over pa's death. He had something come to his stomach.'

'I remember,' Landers said.

'I expect so,' Oak acknowledged.

'All that was over and done with long ago,' Buckley commented, inspecting the photograph – which he was holding in his left hand – then frowning as he glanced down at the letter which he had recently placed on top of the table in order to retain his grip on the gun in his right. 'Where's the silver frame he speaks of? This one looks like a piece of elm to me.'

'Walnut,' Oak corrected, picking up the letter, folding it, and putting it back into his trouser-pocket. 'I don't see a silver frame either. Figures he meant to have the job done, and forgot.'

'Figures,' Buckley agreed, nodding towards Oak's pocket. 'But he speaks in that letter as if he had had the job done.'

Oak shrugged. 'Don't they say the road to hell is paved with good intentions?'

'Some such nonsense,' the sheriff allowed. 'Now we come to that "do" you were on about just now. I'm going to have to place you in custody, Oak, pending further investigations. I expect to charge you with murder some time tomorrow.' He grinned cruelly. 'You know what that means. If you were born to hang, you can't escape the gallows.'

Oak kept his temper on the tightest rein. 'You've heard my story; you've read my letter.'

'You've admitted to being a storyteller,' Buckley jeered. 'You don't have a witness to any word you've told me.'

'But it's a mess of circumstantial evidence, Sneed.'

'You're a prisoner, Oak!' the lawman snapped. 'I don't want any more of the Sneed stuff. You can call me sheriff, and that will stretch to Mr Buckley. But not any further. Got it?'

'Yes, sir.'

'That's acceptable too,' the sheriff said flatly.

'Does it go for Landers too?' Oak mocked again.

'Just the same.'

'You boys have surely got big!'

'Any more of that, Oak, and we'll put you in irons.'

'All right, Sheriff,' Oak sighed. 'What do you want?'

'Your gunbelt first,' Buckley answered. 'Pass it to my deputy.'

Oak unbuckled his gunbelt. He let it swing down to full length from his right hand. Then he held the rig out to Tod Landers, who took it and swung it across his left shoulder.

'Now walk out to your horse,' Buckley ordered, putting the photograph of the prisoner's mother back in the drawer from which it had been taken and pushing the boxwork shut. 'One false move, Oak, and it'll be the worse for you.'

'There's more to this somehow,' Oak said thoughtfully. 'I know there is. You shouldn't have been protecting Pete Brett.'

'Tell it to your lawyer,' Buckley counselled in a bored voice. 'He won't believe a word of it. Out!'

Oak stepped outside. He began walking towards the front gate. Buckley and Landers lagged a step or two behind him. He was aware that the former was managing his removal from the house improperly, and he also sensed that this was deliberate. The sheriff was tempting him to make a run for it. That way he would declare his own guilt and provide Buckley with the chance to shoot him like a dog. Well, there was indeed no escape for a dead man, but time favoured the living. He would behave, and do exactly what he was told to do. There was no problem in that. He had spent the last six years obeying prison guards to the letter, and he still had that state of mind readily on tap.

His easy strides brought him to the gate soon enough. This stood open, and he passed through it, turning to where his horse was tied. He glanced to left and right, in search of the lawmen's mounts, but there was no other horse present, and he supposed that, it being only quarter of a mile into town – and the horse being a relatively noisy brute – the sheriff and his deputy, who had needed to approach George Oak's house as silently as possible, had decided to come out here

on foot. And Buckley confirmed this by saying:
'Lead that crowbait along to my office. We'll be
walking right behind you.'

The horse gave a snort and jibbed a little as its
master caught it at the mouth. 'Why hurt his
feelings?' Oak chided. 'He was the best I could do
on the money I left jail with.'

'Just walk!' Buckley snapped.

Oak did precisely that. He led the brute on
ahead of the badge-wearing pair – passing only
the old black rock-pile on which he had played as
a child en route – and entered town. Coopville was
as dry and dusty as he recalled – and six years
older now – and he gazed about him with a feeling
of dislike as he passed down the rutted way that
served the frame and adobe ugliness of it all. He
came abreast the sheriff's office on the left and at
the centre of the place. Here he halted at the
hitching rail and secured his mount, giving the
animal a consolatory pat as Buckley and Landers
closed in at his back and then bundled him
indoors.

The office was a rather bare and cheerless
place. It had a lime-washed ceiling, paint-licked
walls, and a filth-ingrained floor. The furniture
consisted of just a battered old knee-hole desk and
two straight-backed chairs, while the fittings
covered a gun-rack – without rifles – a bare notice
board, and a pot-bellied stove that was almost
scorched through at the sides. The place reeked of
Mankind, and the smell got worse the closer a
man got to the door of the jailhouse at the back of

it. The prisoner sniffed his disapproval, and would have spat had he dared, for the penitentiary had smelled better than this and the sloth of the incumbent and his deputy was here betrayed.

Nor did Oak's disgust escape notice, and he was given the hardest shake that Landers could manage and made to stand before the desk and turn out his pockets. His money and few other possessions were put into a bag with a drawstring top, and this was thrust into the middle drawer of the desk and shut away. After that Oak was given a pair of threadbare blankets and led into the jailhouse, where he was locked into the third of three cells on the left-hand side of the aisle and informed that the gallows stood in the yard outside his window. 'It's a sight to make a man penitent,' Buckley explained evilly. 'Remember it, when you look out. So this is home sweet home for the time being. Make the most of it, and the town's hospitality. You'll most likely be getting a little place on Boot Hill later on.'

'It don't hurt,' Tod Landers added. 'Didn't your daddy tell you it was quite instantaneous? That's what you told me once when we sat together in school.'

'You wouldn't even know how to spell it,' Oak sneered back.

'I would too,' Landers chuckled. 'H-u-n-g.'

'Oh, go to blazes!' Oak said tiredly.

'No, Bobby – that's where you'll be going soon.'

'He's right,' Buckley said – 'he's right.'

Laughing between themselves, the pair walked

back into the office, one of them shutting the
jailhouse door behind them. Oak pulled a jib after
them, then spread his blankets on the mattress
with which his iron bed was supplied and threw
himself down upon his back, putting his hands
beneath his head and staring up fixedly at the
ceiling.

He couldn't believe that Buckley and Landers
really thought that he had murdered his uncle.
They were just two wicked men bent on
tormenting him. There wasn't anything like
enough evidence against him to secure a death
sentence. He was totally innocent – wholly a
victim of circumstances; that must shine through.
Yet so much that was presented in a court of law
was subject to interpretation. A good lawyer made
all the difference; but he, as a prisoner seeking
legal aid – since he simply couldn't pay for counsel
of his own – would be sure to get some worn-out
old shyster who'd provide a second rate defence.
Events could be made to look ugly; he'd already
seen that for himself. But the most disconcerting
part of all was that the sheriff and his deputy
actually appeared to want him hanged. Why
should they hate him so much? Because of that
business up in Colorado? No, they didn't really
give a damn about that. So was it entirely
personal? There had never been any love lost
between him and the other two, but that was a
situation that repeated millions of times the world
over. You had to hate a guy for the blackest of
reasons to want to see him dead, and he had never

given Buckley or Landers cause to hate him that much. What was left then? Did he stand between them and something they wanted? That one seemed to make no sense at all. His absence from these parts during the last six years appeared to preclude anything of that kind. Beyond all that, there was just perversity and the atmosphere of the day. He could make no sense of anything.

But he was tired – tired right through; he hadn't realized how tired until he had stretched out on this bed. He had come a long way on horseback in a short time, and found it hard to sleep rough. He yawned, and his eyes fell shut. Whatever the future held, they weren't going to hang him today. His mind emptied, and his body went limp. He sank into a deep and peaceful sleep.

Then, he could not say how much later – but he knew it was a long while – he was awakened by the ringing and rattling of metal on metal; and, jolting back to full consciousness far too suddenly, he sat up and gazed towards the door of his cell, seeing that it stood open and Deputy Sheriff Todd Landers was lounging against the bars adjacent and running a tin mug back and forth across their rounded surfaces. 'What –?' Oak began thickly, convinced that he was beset by disaster bloody and absolute.

Landers smiled thinly. 'Out of it. You're free.'

Oak could only gape at the man. 'You're joshing!' he declared stupidly.

'Nope,' the deputy responded.

Leaving his bed, Oak stood there, scrubbing at his eyes and yawning. Would you believe it? Right now this life of his seemed to got up and down like a seesaw.

Three

Leaving his cell, Oak shambled out of the jailhouse and into the office beyond. He was still yawning, and his mind remained befogged by surprise and sleep. It occurred to him then that the light coming in through the windows was the evening light, and that he must have slept a fair piece of the day away. While he felt sure that the rest had done him good in the long term, he only hoped that it had left him up to managing his affairs in the short; for, apart from the larger facts which dominated his changed situation, he seemed almost incapable of putting two sensible thoughts together at the moment.

Oak stepped up to the desk. Sneed Buckley was sitting behind it on one of the room's two straight-backed chairs. The sheriff had tipped his seat onto its rear legs, and he had drawn up one booted foot to rest on the knee of the other limb. Oak's gunbelt and the bag containing his possessions lay on the desktop before the lawmen.

Buckley said: 'You're a lucky man, Oak.'

'Once in a while,' Oak allowed doubtfully.

'What's happening?'

'Didn't Tod Landers tell you?'

'Sure, he told me. You're letting me out.'

'Don't you want to go?'

'That's a damnfool question to ask!' Oak snorted.

'Then why do you ask what's happening?'

'Because I want to know.'

'But you do know.'

Oak groped about inside his head, only too aware that the sheriff had twigged his sleep-befuddled wits and was enjoying the opportunity to confuse him still more. 'G'dammit, I want to know what's behind what I know!'

'A pretty girl.'

'Is it me?' Oak inquired, rubbing the back of his neck and supposing that he must look as big and dense to the smart alecky lawman as he presently felt to himself.

'Heidi Schirmer.'

'Old Schirmer's daughter. She's a pretty kid all right. But what's she got to do with me?'

'Heidi's a woman now. As to your question – Why, I don't rightly know.'

'Thank God there's something you don't know!'

'Didn't I ask if you had a witness to what had happened to you at your uncle's house?'

'How could I have had, blast it?'

Buckley scowled. 'You watch yourself, Bob. I don't rise that fast this time of day, but I can still get snotty if a man gets snotty with me.' He glanced round Oak's right shoulder. 'You tell him, Tod.'

'It's true, Bob,' Landers hastened. 'It seems Miss

Heidi was looking out from behind the pile of black rock which stands beside the trail between here and your uncle's place. She saw you tie your hoss and walk up to the house. Then she saw you throw yourself down when them shots were fired through the door. After that she saw you bust your way in.'

'She also saw somebody leave the back of the house ahead of you,' Buckley added, 'and disappear among the trees on the slope below the ridge. She believes she saw whoever it was on the crest, for just a moment, a minute or two later. But she isn't too certain about that – though it fits okay with what you told us concerning those cut up boots.'

'A guy in a grey shirt and sand-coloured breeks.'

'You say that.'

'Well, I wasn't sure either,' Oak admitted. 'What was Heidi Schirmer doing behind those rocks?'

'Watching for you.'

'No!'

'That's what she told me and Tod this afternoon,' Buckley said, deferring to his deputy again by raising an eyebrow.

'She sure did,' Landers affirmed. 'She was in the habit of going in to do a bit for George Oak now and again. I don't have to tell you her ma, Else Schirmer – God rest her – was pally with George years ago. There were whispers that Oak might have – Well, y'know what I mean. Schirmer had been married twice before getting wed to Else, and he'd been a failure all his life at fatherin' kids. 'Twas said –'

'I know what was said,' Oak interrupted. 'That story was discredited years ago. There's no word of truth in it. Heidi's pure Schirmer. She always did have a soft spot for Uncle George – no doubt on account her mother did before her. He was a real old dog with the women, but he didn't get to so many as all that. Else was straight enough, Tod. She washed and cleaned – no more.'

'I suppose you've better cause to know than most,' the sheriff observed reasonably enough.

Oak was wide awake now, and not unnaturally intrigued. 'It sure tickles me, though. Little Heidi watching for me. It's plain Uncle George told her I'd likely be coming this way.'

'That's how it was,' Buckley said. 'She came in here, and her eyes flashed and she stamped her foot. She informed us she'd heard in town that we'd got you behind bars on suspicion of murder, and she was ready to swear out a statement as to what she'd seen – and kick up a rumpus – if we didn't free you.' His face hardened. 'Not that I could allow myself to be talked to like that by a chit of a girl. And I may as well tell you here and now, Oak, that I'm not happy about letting you out. But I did what I deemed sensible, and went and called on Judge Rod Hailey. I set out the facts before him, and he asked me a heap of questions; and when he'd done – regardless of the fact you were out on parole – he ordered me to release you immediately. Which brings us back to what a lucky guy you are – doesn't it?'

Oak nodded slowly. 'I must thank that girl for her good offices.'

'If you think you should,' Buckley responded. 'But I wouldn't make a big thing of it. Adolf Schirmer never did like you. He's over eighty now, and as cantankerous as all-get-out. I heard him say that Colorado ought to have hanged you for the Jack Royal shooting. Do you figure a call from you would be welcome at the house of such a man? You'd only embarrass his daughter, and it might be foolish to read too much into her part.'

'I've no romantic notions of it,' Oak disclaimed, lying just a tiny bit. 'But she was watching for me, Sheriff, and it has the look of an established thing. She was ready to kick up a fuss for me too.'

Buckley twitched a shoulder. 'So what? She's a girl who knows right from wrong and likes to help.'

'She'd have done the same for anybody, eh?'

The sheriff let his propped boot thud to the floor. 'Your affair, Oak. I've said what I felt I ought to say. How you go on from there is up to you.' He glanced at Landers again. 'Fair, Tod?'

'Fair.'

'There's your gunbelt and the rest,' Buckley said. 'Your horse is still standing at the rail outside.'

Picking up his gunbelt, Oak swung it about his waist and latched it in place. Then he emptied out the bag containing his smaller possessions, putting his money in one trouser-pocket and the odds and ends in the other. Finally, lifting a finger in salute, he made for the street door, but hesitated on opening it and looked back. 'My uncle?'

'His body is with the coffin maker.'

'The house?'

'Locked up. I have the key.'

'The photograph of my mother?'

'You can have it at a later date. I can't promise when.'

'That's no help.'

'You're free, aren't you?'

Compressing his lips, Oak nodded curtly and went out onto the street, shutting up behind him; and then he walked to his horse and stood beside it, trying to make up his mind what to do next.

The sensible part of him begged to be heard. It advised him to cut the possibility of future losses by leaving town straightaway. But the perverse side of him was clamorous. It bawled at him not to forget that his uncle had been foully done to death, that he had suffered considerably because of it, and that revenge and the family honour were not to be discounted.

There remained the matter of Heidi Schirmer too. Despite Sneed Buckley's discouragement, he meant to see and thank Heidi before long. He was curious about the woman she had grown into, and truly grateful for the trouble to which she had put herself in order to get him out of jail. He had been brought up to believe that a simple 'thank you' was the one proof of gratitude that should never be omitted, and Heidi had the right to hear the words from his lips.

But he would not go round to the Schirmer home just now. After dark would do. The chances were that Heidi's aged parent would seek his bed long before she did. Perhaps they would be able to have an hour together, and maybe he would learn the last of Uncle George's mind through her. He was pretty sure that she would advise he take off in the morning, and probably he would. Though God alone knew where. But the world was full of human tumbleweeds like him, and life's wind never ceased to blow. He would fetch up somewhere and prosper. Just see if he didn't!

Yet what for now? He passed his tongue around his gums and the insides of his cheeks. He was about as thirsty as a man could get, and he'd swear his mouth was turning to leather. He needed a drink. Had he been on the trail, the muddy contents of his canteen would have had to suffice; but right now he was in town – still had a few dollars in his pocket – and did not think he should regard a glass or two of light beer as an extravagance. He'd ride up the street to the Golden Bough saloon. Proprietor Jim Simms had always kept his barrels nice and cold, and Oak doubted if six years would have changed that.

Freeing his horse, he stepped into the saddle, then turned away from the law office and began trotting up the street, arriving outside the Golden Bough within the minute. Here he swung down and tied his mount once more, then stepped across

the boardwalk and into the saloon, an atmosphere
heavy with tobacco smoke and the acrid tang of
alcohol meeting him like a smothering cloud; and
he was reminded that the pleasures of vice
required endurance.

Going up to the bar – with its cut-glass back,
erotic paintings, and carved wood – he ordered a
large beer; and, having paid for and received his
drink, turned and faced into the room. While
drinking deeply from the mug in his right hand,
he propped himself on the divide with his left
elbow and relaxed. The beer was as cold and good
as he remembered, and the gaiety around him
revived his spirits. He smiled to himself in the
knowledge that he had acquired an education of a
sort in this place by the time he was eighteen.
Certainly, he had learned the best – and the worst
– about women in here; for Jim Simms had prided
himself on keeping a girl to suit every taste on his
staff. Plump and naughty, slim and pretty, or just
plain homely and willing, you could find them all
in the Golden Bough. Simms had established his
policy in Eighteen sixty and, like the quality of his
beer, it had altered very little since. There were
girls everywhere; they were drifting down from
the balcony in pairs. The rustle of petticoats
thrilled, and the glimpse of garter stunned. Oak
was reminded of how long he had lived without
women, and he found himself idly making his
selection from the talent on display, when a lean,
handsome man of more than six feet in height,
who was clad in a grey shirt and sand-coloured

trousers, entered through a side door and sat down in the empty place at a corner card table – the dealer beginning his deal now that the tall fellow's apparently restored presence completed the school.

Oak straightened out of his lounging posture, and the quietness died inside him. Tense and angry again, he recognised Pete Brett, his old enemy, in the man dressed in the grey shirt and reddish-brown trousers. Though he could prove nothing – and knew that it would be madness to start making accusations – he was instinctively certain that he was looking at his uncle's murderer. Then, as his emotions tightened and his stare grew more intense, the fact of his presence seemed to communicate itself to Brett, who jerked his face round and matched Oak's gaze, forehead notching at the centre and lips twisting viciously. 'Blast you!' Oak mouthed; and, though the words came out almost silently, the fact of them was enough.

Brett turned to the man on his left, a bullet-headed, pudgy-faced brute, with soulless blue eyes under his close-cropped blond hair and the torso of a gorilla. Now Brett spoke a few words, twitching his head towards the bar, and the brute – one of Coopville's infamous Milligan twins, Ray and Joey – reached across the green baize of the tabletop and gave his equally unprepossessing brother a prod in the shoulder, hissing out words through his thick, immobile lips that caused the second man to screw his head round and pick out the watcher at the divide, his expression hardening at once into a readiness for trouble. Then Brett spoke a few words more, a jerk of his chin finally directing, and the Milligan twins rose from their chairs – shorter men than might have been expected – and started crossing the room towards the bar, their tombstone teeth glistening in anticipation and their thumbs tucked behind the buckles of their gunbelts.

Oak felt the urge to run, and knew it would be wisest. The knowledge that it was imperative he stay out of trouble that might involve the law was also a powerful deterrent; but he had his pride, and he knew that he was good enough. He studied the oncoming twins, certain that a fight was now unavoidable, but he was determined that he would neither pull first nor strike the first blow and, though he set his beer aside, he put a smile on his face and continued standing easy. 'Hi, boys!' he greeted. 'Something I can do for you?'

'You son-of-a-bitch!' the Milligan on the right exploded, as the two men halted just in front of their intended victim.

'I think I must have heard you wrong,' Oak said, keeping his smile in place, though his eyes chilled a trifle. 'I never could tell you pair apart. Which one is Ray?'

'I'm Joey,' the Milligan on the left said with an air of self-importance.

'Then you must be Ray,' Oak said to the man who had already addressed him. 'They used to say, when we were kids, you were the twin with the larger mouth and smaller brain. Not that I ever heard there was much in it between you boys where anything was concerned.'

The Milligans reached for their guns, but Oak had his revolver out and cocked before they could even start their draws. 'No, lads,' he said. 'It would be easy to kill you – and that's what you deserve – but there'd be hell to pay afterwards; and I've already paid hell my share. Get back to your card game, and tell Pete Brett I want to talk to him. At that empty table there. The one on the right of the batwings.'

'Pete don't wanna talk to you,' Ray Milligan growled. 'He says you ain't welcome in this town. We don't want killers around. We was to ask you to leave.'

'Ask me?' Oak queried. 'Oh, I think I understand. You couldn't carry a hard thought like that one all the way from there to here. Why, it must be all of twelve paces. Shame on Pete for expecting it.'

'He won't talk to you,' Ray Milligan insisted.

'Tell him to force himself!' Oak ordered, all the banter now gone from his tones.

A shot rang out. The pistol sprang from Oak's grasp. It came down near the end of the bar on his left and spun wildly on its cylinder. Shaking his numbed fingers, Oak looked to where Pete Brett was sitting and saw that the man now held a smoking Colt in his right hand. 'That was a foolish one, Pete!' he called, casting a disapproving glance about him; for, though the middle of the floor had cleared the moment the trouble began, there remained plenty of people around for a ricocheting slug to threaten. 'Never shoot a gun indoors. Isn't that the rule?'

'You've got some right to talk about big mouths!' Brett shouted back. 'What's far worse, you're a dirty rotten killer! You arrive in Coopville, and immediately a man dies! Your own uncle! Show him the door, boys!'

The Milligan twins lunged at Oak, Ray pumping a fist at the taller man's solar plexus. Oak got his left elbow down and blocked the punch, shooting his right mitt into Joey Milligan's face and probably breaking the man's nose. Joey went down, rolling ponderously on his buttocks, and his legs sprawled wide apart. Ducking under a roundhouse swing from Ray, Oak booted Joey where the kick was guaranteed to do the most harm, and the lesser of the twins shrieked with agony and crawled under a nearby table, gathering up his legs and lying there on his side, out of the battle for a certainty.

'That weren't sportin', you varmint!' Ray Milligan raved, closing his eyes and thrusting out his chin as he hooked for Oak's jaw.

'Nor's two against one,' Oak reminded, dodging the other's flying fists and flattening Ray's ears for him. 'This is more like it. Don't you think?'

'Why, you –!' Ray Milligan bellowed, measuring off another haymaker.

Oak parried the blow with his left arm, then crossed with his own right fist. The punch landed

on target, and would have torn a lesser jaw off its
owner's head, but Ray Milligan merely shuddered
down to his toenails and kept bulling in.

Letting go a succession of straight lefts, Oak
kept jolting his man and was content to let the
facial damage accumulate and the punishment
wear Ray down, but suddenly he glimpsed new
movement at Pete Brett's table and realized that
he had better speed things up before the men from
the other end of the room reached him and he was
overwhelmed.

He walked into Ray Milligan, banging his fists
wrist-deep into his opponent's belly without
caring that his punches were several inches low.
Ray began to wobble, hurt to the limit of what he
could take, and Oak kicked him in the side of the
left knee and brought him down into a kneeling
position. Dazed and helpless, the great brute
hung there, and Oak struck from the left with all
his force, the blow knocking Ray onto his side and
spinning him across the floor to join his brother
under the table adjacent.

It was time to treat discretion as the better part
of valour – time to get out of the Golden Bough
pronto; but, glancing towards the street exit, Oak
perceived that he had already left it too late; for a
couple of Pete Brett's cronies had run down the
further side of the room and come round to place
themselves between him and the batwings. The
two men were brandishing beer bottles and looked
mean enough to chop him down, regardless of the
damage that the broken glass might do him. He

must avoid the pair if he could, and he spent a
split second in studying the spread of the other
figures advancing on him, seeking a weak spot,
and he saw one to his right, where a man who was
smaller and older than the average of those who
meant him harm was holding at the end position
in the wing of three men running at him from that
side.

With his left palm thrust out before him, Oak
launched himself at the older man. He caught the
guy full in the face and shoved him aside. Passing
through the space which he had thus made for
himself, Oak headed for the side door from which
he had seen Pete Brett enter the bar a few
minutes ago. Yells went up, turns were completed, and men dived at him. They made every
effort to bring him down, but he eluded their
hands without much difficulty and, his brain
working even faster than his limbs, tipped tables
and chairs into his wake as he came to them. This
caused the pursuit to congest and muddle behind
the chaos that he had produced across the floor.

He reached the door which he had in view.
Screwing at the knob, he flung it open; then,
darting through the exit, he slammed the
woodwork back into place behind him. He saw
now that he was in the open air – in an alley, in
fact, which connected the saloon's back yard with
the street – and he was ready to make the obvious
move and turn left, prior to fleeing for the rear of
the premises and the lots beyond, when he saw a
lovely flaxen-haired girl appear in the townward

side of the alley and beckon vigorously in the direction of the nearby street. 'This way, Bob!' she urged. 'This way!'

Oak was glad to accept her guidance. He turned right and prepared to follow her lead.

Four

Convinced that he must think literally in terms of preserving life itself, Oak pelted after the girl – and was amazed when she stopped after a stride or two and jerked open a door set in the wall of the saloon to her right. She sprang through the aperture and, knowing that he was required to follow suit, Oak did the same on catching up, and she shut the door again and they stood together, softly panting, in the darkness of what from its smell was a coal-house.

Oak could feel the hair bristling on his nape, and nerves were tingling all over him, while a shiver flickered feverishly beneath the heat that his body had generated. They were playing a dangerous game, and had just taken an awful chance. His entire escape from the bar had been built around fractions of a second, and his eruption into the evening light – regardless of the scatterings with which he had cluttered his wake – could have occurred only moments ahead of a similar emergence by his enemies. So the possibility that he and the girl had been glimpsed

while seeking refuge in the coal-house could not
be disregarded. He could make no judgment on
this, since he had not actually looked back
towards the doorway through which he had
escaped from the bar-room before entering here.

Well, they could only hold still and wait. They
would soon find out if their hiding place had been
twigged. Remaining utterly taut, Oak listened
intently to the passage outside – half expecting
the door to burst open suddenly and a sixgun to be
thrust into his face – but, after an age that was in
fact no more than five seconds long, he picked up,
from off to the left, a muffled rush of feet heading
for the back yard and then the rasping splutter of
a few others passing the coal-house door, which
suggested that the pursuers had broken unevenly
on leaving the bar and that the larger part of the
hunt had headed for the lots while the smaller
had made for the main street. Anyway, there
could be no doubt that the uncertainty betrayed
by the division meant that Oak and his
companion had not been spotted while hiding
themselves, and that the girl's obvious belief that
the pursuers would never dream that the fugitive
would risk concealing himself at a spot so near the
start of the chase could prove a winner. 'Where
the heck did you spring from, Heidi?' he
whispered; for the blonde was old Schirmer's
daughter – and he had recognised her from the
first moment.

'I'd been watching the law office,' Heidi
murmured in response – 'waiting for Sneed

Buckley to free you. I saw you leave the law office, and hoped you'd come towards me; but, being the same old Bob, you had to make the saloon your first port of call, and I was obliged to follow. I kept peeping into the Golden Bough through a window, and saw the mess you were getting yourself into. I became mighty afraid for you, Mr Oak.'

'You and Mr Oak both,' Oak breathed wryly. 'I can guess the rest. Your wit is sharper than mine. Thanks for all you've done on my behalf since I hit town.'

'We're not out of the wood yet, Bob.'

'I guess we'll have to hang on in here for a bit,' he agreed. 'Let things die down. I didn't mean to leave town without dropping in on you. I was going to do it later. On account of your pa.' Her silence was uncomprehending, so he added: 'I hoped he would be in bed, and the coast clear. Old Adolf has no time for me.'

'He doesn't like anybody much,' Heidi sighed. 'He's deaf as a post now, and spends most of his life upstairs in his room. That leaves me to do pretty much as I please. It's not a good life, but it might be worse.'

'You can be a prisoner without going to jail,' Oak acknowledged. 'Not that I'd recommend the Big House to anybody.'

'Bob, you're a fool!'

'Yeah?'

'It's time somebody told you.'

'Exactly what?'

'You've got a fiddlefoot, a reckless way, and a

hot temper,' she informed him. 'You'll swing before you've done.'

'I know what this is all about,' he gritted. 'I've done a few things I'm ashamed of, Heidi, but I've never killed except in self-defence. That business with the tinhorn was a case in point.'

'What were you doing in his game?' she demanded softly. 'Did anybody force you into it?'

'No.'

'Then whatever happened to you was your own fault,' the girl declared. 'We've got far more control over what comes to us than we think.'

He couldn't say that she was wrong – because he knew that she was right. 'Heidi, life is for the living. Prairies are to cross, hills to climb, and rivers to ford. It's got to move, honey. It's got to go forward. We *have* to make it happen.'

'There's just as much life here in Coopville as there is anywhere else.'

'For somebody who lights on Coopville,' Oak agreed.

'You think that's smart.'

'Plainly you don't.'

'I don't.'

'I still thank you for what you've done for me.'

'I've always liked you, Bob!' she protested, her whisper developing a dangerous twang. 'There's much about you that is real nice, and you'd do well if you didn't go into places that are downright nasty. You're calling down destruction on your own head. That's a silly waste!'

'Hush!' he breathed. 'It's no big deal, Heidi. You

always did overdo it. Figures – with all the
watching I've heard about – you want to talk to
me about something more important than this.'

'I sure do,' she admitted. 'That can wait until
we're safe, and I've got you home.'

They kept silent after that, and time went by.
There was just the darkness, the tiny chinks of
light around the coal-house door, and the soft
rhythm of their breathing. But there was, of
course, noise without. A dog barked sporadically,
a waggon rumbled just audibly at the edge of
town, and there was a chinking of glass nearby.
Then there came sounds that could only presage
the hunters returning to the bar, and these were
followed by a banging of doors. After that an
approximate hush descended, and all incoming
noises seemed increasingly muted. Now something appeared to snap, and Oak said with
finality: 'We've been in here long enough.'

Heidi opened the door slowly, then peered
around its outer edge. 'It's all right,' she mouthed,
turning her face towards Oak and nodding.

They stepped out into the passage, and Heidi
closed up silently behind them. Then she tiptoed
towards the end of the alley that served the street.
Oak followed at her heels, but now he did look
back, praying that no hostile face would appear in
their wake.

Nothing untoward occurred. They paused at the
limit of the narrow way, and the girl did some
more peeping out. 'Okay,' she said after a
moment.

They walked out onto the street. Here they
turned left, then hurried along the sidewalk
towards the western edge of Coopville. Presently
they reached the largest of the few brick-built
houses in town. This was owned by Adolf
Schirmer, and Heidi opened the front door and let
them in. They passed down the hall and into the
back of the house, entering the comfortable
kitchen there, and the girl pointed to an armchair
beside the hearth and said: 'I'll make a pot of
coffee. It does a man more good than beer.'

Oak had his doubts about that, but he was
careful not to voice them, and he sat down, with
head politely inclined, and made a steeple of his
fingers. Then he looked on while his fair-haired
companion cheered up the fire and put a kettle of
water on to boil. 'That filthy coal!' she exclaimed
as, with her immediate task done, she bent
forward, her breasts filling the front of her yellow
dress and her bustle tipping high, to examine a
black mark on the garment's hem.

'A coal-hole is no place to spend half an hour
with a real pretty girl,' Oak commented, tongue in
cheek, 'and never a kiss.'

'You can stop that, Bob Oak!' she informed him.
'I've heard all about you from the girls. You're
going to be as bad as your uncle if you don't watch
out!'

'Don't all women have a secret fancy for men
like that?' Oak inquired, an outrageous mer-
riment dancing in his eyes.

'Bobby,' she said seriously, 'I'm your cousin by

blood. Yes, George Oak was my real begetter. Mother told me before she passed away. It was only the once she dishonoured Schirmer, and I was the result.'

'And there I was defending the old goat a few hours ago!' Oak snorted, making no secret of his disgust. 'I didn't think he could have done a thing like that. But I guess he brought your ma to it somehow. I'm sorry Heidi. Truly sorry.'

'I'm not,' she said. 'I know who I am, and what I'm here for. George Oak, Adolf Schirmer; should a girl worry who her father is?' Heidi shrugged. 'I'm going to live my life, Bob, and feel I've had all there is when my turn comes to die. As for mother – Well, I'm woman enough to know it takes two to make a bargain. I'm not going to blame her, and you mustn't have regrets.'

'Uncle George knew?'

'Of course he did.'

'Was that what you wanted to talk to me about?'

'No,' she replied. 'I didn't even intend to mention it. It all came from the way you were looking at me just now.'

'We're only cousins,' he said. 'Cousins often –'

'I know what cousins do,' she cut in, 'and I wouldn't mind. But I'm not going to. So don't try it on, Bobby.'

'Wouldn't dream of it,' he assured her. 'But if you wouldn't mind –'

'I'm the result of a woman's hour of weakness,' she reminded. 'I'm not going to give history the chance to repeat itself. Nevertheless, what I want to talk to you aboout does concern us both, and very much so.'

'You've got me interested, Heidi.'

Crimping off a smile, she left the room – going into the parlour across the hall – and he heard her open a drawer and begin rummaging around; but she soon returned to the kitchen, carrying in her hands a silver-framed photograph. 'I was asked to give you this,' she said. 'George Oak couldn't have had any idea that he was going to be murdered when he passed it to me; but, sad as his death must be, this may have turned out for the best.'

Bob Oak took the photograph from her. He studied it for several moments, frowning to himself. 'So Uncle George had a second photograph of my mama. I guess that explains much. The law dug out the one I'd always known over at the house today, and it was the same as ever, yet Uncle George had told me in a letter that he'd had it framed in silver. This is beautiful. It's mama as a really young woman.'

'She was Doris Saunders then,' Heidi responded. 'George Oak told me all about it. You can guess, can't you? It's the common story. Doris Saunders preferred your pa. George Oak might have been a better man if she had not.'

'And you might not have been here.'

'We've been into that, Bob.'

'Well, I'm glad as hell you are.'

Heidi reached forward, pointing. 'The cardboard backing is made to slip out of the frame. Slide it away, Bob.'

He moved to her bidding, then hesitated.

'You're wondering why. You'll see.'

His hands too large for the job, Oak began bending the carboard into a position from which its removal from the back of the frame clearly ought to be easy, but he was still showing a want of dexterity, when he heard a window fly open upstairs and a cracked male voice shout down in equally fractured English: 'Vat you do down there, hey, Pete Brett? You gid away from my house, jugen schweinehund!'

'That's pa yelling!' Heidi breathed, her face turning pale. 'Somebody must have seen us come here. Either that or Brett and the others must have realized that you could have come to me for help.'

'Gid away!' the voice upstairs insisted. 'Gid away!'

'The cave!' the girl said, going to the back door and silently opening it. 'You remember the cave. Go there! I'll come to you later.'

Oak had time neither to think nor argue. Discovery had to be too near for that. Indeed, it might be just outside the back wall. But Oak knew he would have to chance that and dived out through the exit, giving the blonde neither word nor glance in passing. Then, taking to the path which ran between the two rough-dug garden patches, he hurried towards the foot of the property, dodging off to the right and seeking cover as he heard heavy footfalls round either end of the house behind him and approach the back door.

Conscious of a dusky gloom now enclosing him,

Oak fetched up behind a shed that he judged,
from the piles of horse manure lying near near it,
was used as a stable. Moving back to the corner
that he had just turned, he shoved the photograph
of his mother into the top of his trousers and
peeped out, seeing that Ray and Joey Milligan
had just halted outside the Schirmer back door
and begun to beat on the woodwork with the butts
of their drawn guns.

The door opened to the pair, and Oak heard
Heidi speak words of protest. Then he glimpsed
her abrupt retreat before the monstrous twins, as
Ray and Joey forced their way into the kitchen;
but, enraged as he was at the sight of their
bullying shoves, he was compelled once more to
consider himself, for Pete Brett in person
suddenly appeared at the rear of the dwelling and
started to look down the garden path with a
calculating eye.

Oak drew back his head. Brett, as he had every
cause to know – from events past and present –
was a clear-thinking and sensitive man, who
could be relied upon to make a thorough search. It
would be wise to seek a better hiding place than
the present one – in anticipation of the man
coming this way. But where? The lots extended on
either hand, while directly before him – southwards, where he had wished to go – the land
stepped back in low terraces of brown clay and
small rocks, nothing in the form of bushes or other
growth appearing on the first three hundred
yards to break its essential openness.

Craning, Oak cast a rather desperate glance across the ground at his back. He saw a considerable clump of currant bushes there. The growth was thick and green, and the darkness of the earth about its roots suggested that the bushes were regularly watered to encourage a lush crop in the season of the year. Oak eyed the spread of the bushes, reckoning that, in the present fading light, a man might crouch down at their centre and hide safely from any save the closest searcher. But that, of course, was most likely what Brett would prove to be. Still, he'd got to try something and the currant bushes looked his best bet.

Catfooting over to the bushes, Oak sidled to their heart, ignoring the scratches that he picked up. Then he settled onto his heels, the growth virtually closing above him, and began waiting. Nor was he kept long in suspense; for, as a chink of vision revealed, Pete Brett appeared round the further end of the stable only a few moments later, and for one horrible instant Oak thought that the searcher had actually heard him enter the bushes; but Brett's subsequent behaviour showed this to be false, since he tiptoed slowly round the building and then gave a minute to searching inside it – or so the muffled sound of his unseen movements said – before coming back to the rear of the stable and adopting a contemplative stance that still didn't take the presence of the bushes into any real account.

With leg muscles aching and lungs barely

stirring, Oak wished Brett a thousand miles away, but the man seemed to have become rooted. Then, as the other lifted his head and seemed about to walk back to the garden path, a small bird – one of the last still on the forage – dropped out of the dusk and came to rest on a twig directly above Oak's head. That in itself did no more than draw a casual glance from Brett, and was obviously too slight a thing to register any serious meaning in his consciousness. Doubtless his deeper attention would not have been claimed had the bird sat there for a few moments; but, almost certainly unaware of Oak's presence until it was actually down, the little creature gave a sudden chirp of startlement and literally bounced back into flight. Even so, Brett did not appear in any sense alerted, though he did start to close in on the fruit bushes; and there was the rub; for Oak realized that once the man got near enough he must look almost straight down into the fugitive's hiding place and spot him crouching there.

Then a voice from the direction of the house hollered: 'Hey, Pete!'

Brett checked, glancing towards the unseen caller. 'Hello?'

'Where are you?'

'Down here.'

'Where's that?'

'At the bottom of the garden,' Brett shouted back. 'What do you want?'

'Me and Joey have been over the whole house,' came the answer. 'He's nowhere to be found indoors.'

'There's no sign of him down here,' Brett
rejoined.

'Can he have stole a horse from some place and
galloped off?'

'Maybe,' Pete Brett allowed. 'But not from here.
The girl's nag is still in its stall.'

'What are we goin' to do now, Pete?'

Brett did not reply; but, much to the hidden
man's relief, he walked to the garden path and
turned for the house, the presence of the stable
cutting him off from Oak's view almost at once.

Oak remained hunkered down for perhaps
another minute; then, reasonably sure that it was
now safe to do so, he straightened up, pulling a
face as he eased his half locked knees and
stretched his calves. Relieved, he glanced first
into the twilit south, with its fading sky and sepia
contours, and then towards the house, uncertain
as to the right way to go in view of how things had
turned out; but the girl had told him to go to the
cave – and said that she would visit him there
later – so he decided to follow her wishes, fearing
to give her additional worry anyhow, since he
realized that she could be having trouble with her
father about now. Adolf Schirmer, volatile at the
easiest of times, was probably throwing a fit over
the invasion of his home by some of Coopville's
lowest elements, and he might need a lot of
calming down.

Making sure that his mother's photograph was
still safely tucked into his waistband, Oak left the

currant bushes and set off southwards. He kept
low in the shadows, while giving time to working
out the position of the cave which Heidi had
mentioned so vaguely just before he fled from her
kitchen. It would be the one over in the clay banks
to the left of where he was now – opposite the
church spire in fact – a hole that made him
shudder a little to think about it today; for his
adult mind recognised the instability of clay as his
juvenile one had not, and when he recalled some
of the romps that had taken place in there, he
could only thank God that the roof had not fallen
in and left Coopville with a major tragedy.

He found the cave about five minutes later. It
was an oblique slash near the foot of a bank
around twenty feet high. Far smaller than he
remembered, it exhaled the odour of the grave,
and he could not bring himself to enter. Soon he
sank down on a rock to the left of the entrance,
grateful for the chance to rest, and closed his eyes
for a minute – but only a minute, since the
mystery of his mother's photograph was again
exercising his imagination as nothing else had
that day.

Turning to the back of the frame once more, he
made a new attempt to remove the sheet of
cardboard there, and this time managed it easily,
a piece of vellum that was dark and wrinkled with
age falling from behind the photograph and
fluttering to the ground between his feet. He
picked the four inch square of ancient calfskin up
again and held it to what little light was left,

making out a variety of tracings upon it, but it was the words near the top – blocked and unmistakable – that set his heart racing. For they read: *TREASURE HERE*.

Five

Bob Oak's initial surprise quickly passed away. This must have been done in jest. Uncle George had placed this treasure map at the back of the photograph of his nephew's mother as a joke. It was the kind of heavy-handed, humourless type of skit that George Oak had often seemed to regard as amusing. A strong, sensual man, he had not been over-blessed with brains, and he had been far less interested in how a joke might go down over-all than in the fact that it struck him as funny at the moment.

It could even be that Uncle George had thought it would be amusing to see how his jailbird nephew reacted to the possibility of coming by an easy fortune. The man had probably bought a worthless map from some cheating barker at a travelling fair. Yet, with all that perceived and considered, it didn't quite ring true. Yes, Uncle George had had a childish and undeveloped sense of humour, but he had also possessed intelligence enough to know the difference between his own crude idea of fun and actual unkindness. For, if

things were as they appeared to be, there was
unkindness here, since his jest not only mocked
his nephew – who had never done anything other
than hold him in regard – but it had seemingly
duped his illegitimate daughter also; as, from her
manner when she had put the photograph into
Bob Oak's hands, Heidi had apparently shared
the same kind of excitement which had recently
arisen in him.

There was likewise the chance, of course – and
perhaps much the better chance – that George
Oak had himself been mistaken as to the
credibility of the map. Indeed, he could even have
been at the end of a chain of people who had
passed on this particular map for one reason or
another for many a year – some totally deceived,
perhaps, and others merely doubting. But all that
was woolly speculation, and there was no denying
that the thing did have a certain look and
atmosphere of authenticity about it. The vellum
was genuinely old, and the inking and shape of
hand upon it suggested an earlier and less
copperplate-minded time of day than the present
one.

Bob Oak tried to give the map his entire eyes
and mind, but the light was now much too far
gone to let him pore over it as he wished. He had
matches in his pocket, but did not dare strike one
out here in the open for fear that the abrupt
glimmer of flame might be seen at a distance. So,
though it went against the grain, he scrambled
into the cave adjacent and crawled into the back

of the oppressive hole; where, crouched under a lowering roof, he took out and fired a match, first reversing the flame to make it flare and then holding it vertically to achieve the slowest possible consumption of the burning stick.

Quickly spreading the map out with his left hand, Oak let the matchlight shine upon it. He could at first make no sense of what he saw, and burned up three matches before he grasped that the two very closely parallel lines drawn down the middle of the vellum were meant to represent the banks of the Rio Grande. Indeed, when he came to look closer still, he saw that the tracings had been minutely inscribed at their base with the more correct Mexican name of Rio Bravo. And with that much established, the rest of what was present fell easily into shape – with the corrugations on the left of the river undoubtedly marking the Black Range and the cross towards the lower end of the mountains, initialled SR, providing the approximate position of Santa Rita.

Somewhat below the town – though the true distance was impossible to calculate, since the orientation of the map was established entirely on the line of the river and any required distance would have to be worked out from the lines of latitude and longitude on a properly scaled atlas – were printed the words Mission of S. Miguel, and over these, arrowed by the *TREASURE HERE* caption from above, was a Christian cross. This surmounted a block of some kind, and could not be confused with the cross formed by the intersection of oblique ines which marked Santa Rita.

Flicking out what was left of his current match, as it started to burn his fingers, Oak sat there in the dark, sucking absently at his scorched cuticle. The map was, to say the least of it, an inadequate tracery, and yet, disregarding the great distances and immense terrain that it reduced to nothing, it contained all the basic detail required by a search.

If he had read what was present correctly – and he didn't see how he could have got it far wrong – the treasure mentioned on the map had been concealed in the Mission of San Miguel. Not that that conveyed too much to Oak just then, since he had never before heard of the place; but then – aside from not being a religious man and having little interest in the country's Spanish past – there were scores of Jesuit missions in New Mexico of which he had never heard. Anyway, finding Santa Rita would be no more difficult than following the valley of the Rio Grande south-wards, and it went without saying that, proximity having been established, locating the mission itself should prove no impossible task. If the map's credibility could be established – and he had the feeling now that it was crude enough to be real – he certainly had the time at this stage of his life to put into the treasure hunt that it seemed Uncle George had wanted him to undertake, for nothing mattered much to him today; but even so he could not set off into that southern yonder without first establishing that his efforts would be spent on a true purpose. Yet how did a man confirm validity in a case like this? He saw no way. A lot of faith was required, and Oak had never had too much of that in anything.

Thus he remained pondering at the back of the cave for the next hour or more. Then, suddenly feeling a tremor of panic at being too tightly enclosed, he scuttled swiftly out of the cave and stood in the cool air beneath the brightness of the stars, a finger lifted to the trickle of sweat on his left temple and his lungs inflating gratefully. And he was still savouring the night and the space about him, when he heard light footfalls hurrying towards him from the direction of the town.

'Bob?' came Heidi's muted call a few moments later.

'Over here.'

She homed in on the sound of his voice. 'Sorry I've been so long.'

'I've had plenty to occupy my mind,' he responded.

'You've opened the back of your mother's photograph?'

'Yes,' he said, remembering now that he had left the silver frame and picture itself lying beside the rock on which he had sat down on coming to this spot.

'What do you think?'

'You answer that one, Heidi.'

'I think it's real.'

'Likely,' Oak conceded. 'Where did that map come from? Did Uncle George buy it off some numskull at the fair?'

'No, it was given to him,' the girl answered. 'As a dying gift or – or maybe a sort of payment.'

'How's that again, honey?'

'You remember how George Oak liked to take off buck shooting once in a way,' Heidi said. 'It was a few months back, when he went that last time. As he told me, he came on an Englishman's camp up in the forest. The man had had a bad fall and was clearly dying. George Oak did what he could for the poor fellow, and the pair of them talked about home and folk and doings – all the things you'd expect two men to talk about when one is approaching his end. And why the Englishman was in New Mexico finally came out.'

'Tell me.'

'His folk back in England had lost their money,' she explained, 'and they were having a hard time. They were desperate to find a means of repairing their fortunes. Then one of the family remembered that they had this old treasure map. It went back to the end of the last century, and had been fetched home from America by an ancestor of the dying man's, a Colonel Bayward. It seems the colonel accepted it off an American explorer, a Richard Giles, in payment for goods. The deal took place in Santa Fe. Giles was an old man, and he had run himself right down and wanted to get back to his home in the East while his legs would still carry him. He told Colonel Bayward that the map showed where he had hidden a treasure of great value. This treasure had been accumulated from the natives by Hernando Cortes himself, but the Aztecs had managed to recover it from the Spanish chief and put it in one of their temples.'

'It figures Richard Giles winkled it out of the temple,' Oak said, as the girl paused. 'Over in Mexico.'

'Yes, he stole it over there,' Heidi agreed, 'and he had to leave Mexico in a hurry because of that. Only, of course, this was all Mexico at that time of day.'

'Treasure is mighty heavy stuff to pack around,' Oak hazarded, 'and he was being chased.'

'You've got it exactly,' the blonde acknowledged. 'Richard Giles figured he'd make much better time if he hid the treasure for a less pressing day and devoted all his energy to leaving his pursuers behind. So he made a stop at the Mission of San Miguel and, after making the chance, hid his loot away in a safe place.'

'Can't doubt he meant to return for it at that time,' Oak said, 'so it figures the rest of his escape played hell with him. He must have known he'd never go back by the time he reached Santa Fe and met up with Colonel Hayward. I wonder if our explorer sat down in Santa Fe and drew his map.'

'Nobody will ever know exactly where he did that,' Heidi said. 'It's likely Colonel Bayward didn't believe the treasure story anyway. Perhaps he just did the kindly thing by an old man that he could see was slowly failing. Whatever the truth of that, the colonel didn't head south, so it's quite possible that the treasure is still where Richard Giles tucked it away.' She made a clicking sound with her tongue. 'I do so hope that old man got home. I'd like to think he died beside the sea or wherever he wanted to be.'

'Well, he was an explorer and knew what to expect,' Oak growled. 'All that happened long before the day of the railroad, and while the Indians were still thick as fleas across the country. He could have died any one of ten thousand places.' He sighed abstractedly. 'What I don't get is why Uncle George should have got up to all this monkey business. Having a picture put in a silver frame is an ordinary thing. A picture I didn't actually ask for, hell-and-dammit, though he said I did. That's something else I don't properly follow.'

'What you are forgetting,' Heidi reminded, 'is the involvement of Pete Brett and his pals – and the fact that George Oak was murdered. None of that happened by chance, Bob, and it's all part and parcel.'

'Keep talking.'

'George Oak's last woman was Ethel Brett, Pete's mother,' Heidi again explained. 'George – likely too talkative in bed – told Ethel Brett about the treasure map and how he had come by it. But then he had a quarrel with her and she spoke words that made him realize she was not to be trusted.'

'So?' Oak prompted.

'You were pretty smart just now,' the girl said tiredly, a note of exasperation coming through, 'but now you've gone thick-skulled on me again.'

'If I'm to ride south for the Mission of San Miguel,' Oak said forbearingly – 'which is what I figure Uncle George had in mind for me to do on behalf of him, you, and me – I want first to know all there is to know about what happened at this end. All the tricks and diversions and wrong beliefs and such. Anything that has a place. D'you see?'

'I suppose that is reasonable,' Heidi conceded; 'but it's no more than I've been trying to do for you. George Oak told Ethel Brett that he'd had the map sewn into the sole of one of his boots. Obviously to mislead –'

'That makes it sound like he was afraid something might happen to him,' Oak interrupted. 'You said he wasn't expecting to die when he handed the silver-framed photograph to you.'

'He was afraid he might get robbed by the Bretts,' the girl replied. 'I was afraid of it too. I wouldn't have helped him otherwise. We never dreamed of murder. Who does?'

'It's always other folk who get done to death,' Oak acknowledged. 'It still appears to me I blundered into this at the worst moment possible. At least those sliced open boots are explained, though. I expect Sneed Buckley told you about them.'

'The sheriff said nothing to me about any boots.'

Oak could see there'd been no need, and the law did not discuss details of its cases with members of the public anyhow, so he told her about the pair of ruined boots that he had found on the summit of the ridge behind his uncle's house; but, in view of all that had gone before, it was really an irrelevance and did no more than top off the details of what had happened to Uncle George and the predicament in which Bob Oak realized that he was still enmeshed. 'Y'know, Heidi,' he champed, 'I'm far from sure Sneed Buckley didn't engineer my freedom so that Pete Brett could have a clear run at me and my doings. I wonder if Pete's got something on Buckley? Or maybe it's just the promise of a backhander. Heaven knows! But there's a smell about my release.'

'You're overdoing it again,' Heidi said. 'This is a small town, Bob. When was anything ever a hundred percent straight in a small town?'

'There's no help in that,' Oak grumbled. 'This is one small town I shan't be sorry to put behind me again.'

'You're going south?' she asked tensely. 'There's still no absolute proof that map is genuine.'

'I feel a lot of weight in favour of its being so,' he returned. 'Anyhow, I'm ready to take a chance. Down the other track lie the Owlhoot and tilling the soil. Likely a life short and hectic, or years and years of boredom. I'm none too keen on sweating for pips, honey. I'd rather try to get it all at once – and pay whatever price is asked.'

'Knowing you for what you are,' the blonde said – 'and now that we're right down to it – I think you're right.'

'Fifty-fifty?' he asked.

'I'll be happy with a third. That is what George

Oak intended.'

'Fifty-fifty,' Oak said, chuckling briefly. 'It could easily turn out fifty percent of nothing.' He sauntered over to where his mother's photograph lay dismantled in the light of the rising moon. Recovering the picture and the cardboard backing, he replaced them in the silver frame and then passed the whole to his hovering companion. 'Take care of this for me.'

'Have you got the map safe?'

He patted the trouser-pocket into which he had thrust it somewhat absently while thinking matters over so intensely in the cave nearby. 'Now comes the tough part,' he said. 'Or what could be. Getting back that horse of mine. It's standing right slap bang in front of Jim Simms' saloon.'

'I'd have brought you mine,' Heidi said. 'But my pony isn't up to your weight.'

'Being a big guy has its drawbacks,' he admitted. 'Not that that old grulla of mine is up to taking a lot of punishment any more.'

'Would it be less risky if I tried to recover it for you.'

'Let a man do a man's work,' he advised shortly. 'You go home to your father. He wouldn't have much left, would he, if anything happened to you?'

'I guess not,' the girl sighed. 'I just pray God I never grow old and become a trial. I had to dose him up with hot whisky before I came out. He went near loco over Pete Brett and those Milligan twins.'

'Feared it,' Oak growled, 'feared it.' Putting out

a hand, he gripped her right shoulder and shook her gently. 'Be seeing you, Heidi. Watch for me, eh? So long.'

'Farewell, Bob,' she responded, then walked away; and he let the night and the townward country swallow her before he strode off himself, curving out to the right with the intention of following a big arc and entering Coopville from its eastern end.

He moved briskly over the gently terraced land, feeling pretty good – all things considered – and he was reflecting on the benefits of a long sleep in the local jailhouse, when he brought the dimly lighted buildings of the town's eastern boundary into view. After that he located the trail that led towards Texas, followed it inwards, and then began treading the boardwalk on the left of the main street, slowing with every step as he approached the Golden Bough, until he was at the last advancing with extreme caution on the hitching rail at the front of the saloon.

Now he shouldered up to the most westerly angle of the building next to the Golden Bough, peering hard into the pools of inky shadow on either side of the batwings. He glimpsed no movement of any kind. Perhaps he was going to be lucky. Maybe Pete Brett had neglected to identify the fugitive's horse and place a guard to watch it. It looked as if he need only walk up to his mount – which was tossing at the rail, much as he had left it – untie the brute, and then ride away. But, as he was preparing to step out into the street and cross the intervening ground, there was a sudden stirring under the saloon's awning, and the tip of a cigarette appeared and glowed a bright red beside one of the timber uprights.

There was somebody keeping an eye on the horse after all. Brett had not failed to do the obvious. Not that Oak had really supposed he would, and he was thankful that he had remained cautious up to the last instant. But he must not allow himself to be deterred. Things were reasonably in his favour, and he must act. No more propitious moment was coming. He must regain the use of his horse, and it might as well be now.

The guard yonder would have to be knocked cold. Oak hated attacking any man from behind, but he saw no other way in this situation. Directly ahead of him was the mouth of an alley. If he crossed the gap while still deep in the shadow of the buildings to his left, he ought to be able to catfoot along the front of the saloon and to within a few yards of the guard's back before the other realized that he was there. Then, as the man swung round, he should have ample time to let go a punch to the jaw that would render the fellow senseless for several minutes to come.

Crossing the entrance to the narrow way, Oak moved onto the saloon's boardwalk and tiptoed rapidly towards the lounging guard. Everything was going exactly to plan, and he had already wound himself up to release that tremendous straight right, when matters went just as thoroughly wrong, for he tripped where the slats were broken and went floundering into a fall that landed him on his knees and elbows.

The guard spun round, startled. 'Who the –?' he began; but he had undoubtedly guessed, for he whipped out his revolver and made to point it downwards at Oak's head.

Cursing, but unhurt, Oak scrambled off the floor, though remaining in a crouch, for he could see that the other was going to put a bullet in him if he didn't attack there and then; so, driving upwards beneath the guard's gun-arm, he sank his crown into his enemy's solar plexus. The man folded before the contact and went staggering backwards, his gun flashing at the roof.

The shot echoed thunderously, and Oak knew that every vestige of surprise had left him. The occupants of the saloon – and probably the rest of the town – would have been alerted by the explosion. Oak judged that he had only seconds left in which to help himself. Allowing no pause, he went for the guard again, and there, with the man still splay-footed and loose-armed in the oily half-light under the awning, he threw his two hardest punches ever. Both blows connected with the jaw at which they had been aimed, and the guard went down with a thud and lay inert, his Colt springing out of his grasp and bouncing to rest against Oak's left boot.

Oak swept the weapon into his hand. Backing up, he heard shouting voices and lumbering footfalls within the bar. Keeping the bullets down, he blasted three times through the batwings, shattering the ancient cane facings and leaving big holes through which he was able to glimpse something of the panic which his shots had caused within.

Again deeming that a grant of seconds was his, Oak palmed his appropriated weapon away and leaped towards his horse. He came down beside the animal, a hand on the rail. Breaking the tie, he speared his near-side stirrup – the mount starting to circle and snort with fright – then, skipping hard, he forked leather and yanked the brute's head to the left, goading it down the main street at full gallop.

'It's Oak all right!' he heard Pete Brett shout in his wake. 'Get the varmint!'

Pistols cracked and boomed, sending lead within inches of his head and crouched back. Lights came and went on either hand, blurring almost, and the street rang with the echoes of shot and flight.

'Halt in the name of the law!' Sneed Buckley's voice yelled; and the sheriff jumped into the street ahead – and then out of it again.

'Go to hell!' Oak yelled back.

Then there was just the night, and the country, and he was clear and away.

Six

Trotting his mount at a comfortable pace, Oak gazed southwards through the morning light, his eyes aching from the silvery glare off the great bend of the Rio Grande that branded the riverside cow country through which he was passing. It was a glorious morning, vivid in the last degree, with a bird trilling overhead, the smoke of a ranch camp drifting white across the meadow, and the peaks of the San Andres floating above a skyline that was hardly real. Oak was four days out of Coopville, and a hundred and fifty miles down the river from where he had started, and he was so much at peace with himself and the world that he hardly cared for wealth, the love of women, or his own salvation. If a guy had to die right now and become a part of this earthly paradise, he would have all any man could want.

But the exaltation was too spirit-sapping to last, and his inner quiet was soon disturbed. There was this great uncertainty which possessed him. Was he being pursued by Pete Brett and others? How much could Brett be sure that he,

Oak, actually knew? Could the man have any
certainty that his enemy had ridden south in
search of the treasure hidden at San Miguel?
Even allowing that he, Oak again, was equally
unsure of how much Brett knew, he could not see
how the other could be certain of anything at all.
Not even that there had been a truly significant
meeting between Bob and Heidi Schirmer. What
had happened to the treasure map must have
been a mystery to Brett since he had cut open
George Oak's boots and found nothing. He must
have wondered many times if it had a real
existence or whether his mother had simply got
hold of one of George Oak's yarns.

The trouble was that extra something in the
mind of Man. Folk did so much on the spur of
intuition, and Pete Brett's greed would give him
plenty of that. He would be going along with the
feel of things, and that could do harm enough, as
it had always done in the past. What between
petty theft, rolling Saturday night drunks, and
the occasional sale of a rustled cow, Oak had often
thought, when Pete had come nosing along and
demanded his cut of the profits, that Brett's mind
was his own.

Wicked as Oak now perceived it to have all
been, it had seemed no more than a mingling of
fun and irritation when they were teenagers, but
now it was the evil of a grown man with which he
might have to deal. In a way, it was a case of the
past catching up. There was some kind of dreadful
affinity between him and Pete Brett, and he

prayed heaven that it would not be given the chance to develop any further. If it did – here, there, any old where – they would finally come face to face and one of them would kill the other, and he was by no means sure that he was up to killing Pete Brett, who had much better than average skill with a sixgun and was craftier than a bank full of foxes.

But perhaps he was worrying unduly. When a man started losing confidence in himself, he handed power to others. Pete Brett was only human, and damned ignorant with it in many respects. Most probably there was nothing on his backtrail to worry about. Or if pursuers there had been, it was possible that they had asked questions and latched onto one of his false trails before now. Because he was no fool either, and that sidetrack at Jurales had surely made Quemado look like his goal.

Well, he'd be coming to Hillsboro soon and ought to be in Santa Rita by this evening. He could then begin asking discreet questions of his own. After all, there were no mysteries or legends surrounding San Miguel that he had ever heard of and travellers were forever asking the way. All he wanted was to get out of this business with a profit – as quickly as possible, and without harming anybody. If he could do that, he would regard all his recent anxieties as worth the candle. On the other hand, if forced to earn his profit, he was ready for that too. Just so long as there was a profit.

Oak rode on through the morning, and rested at noon. He'd set out with plenty of grub in his bags, and was still picking at it, so the nine dollars and something he'd had in his pocket on fleeing Coopville was still intact and his very meagre insurance policy. Not that a man need starve around here. The country was teeming with game. He could catch himself a fish or shoot a bird almost any time he wanted. Thus he took his siesta under a bush, with the warm earth against his back and the summer in his nostrils and, when the sun slipped west of its flaring zenith, he rose, remounted, and journeyed on, the ribbed core-stone of the Black Range towering above him now and the breeze full of pine scent and rocking butterflies.

It was dark when he entered Santa Rita, and he was again tired and would have been glad to put up in the loft at the horse barn and forget the rest; but he was determined not to waste any of the morrow against something that he could still do today; so he made a round of the saloons on small beer and small talk, asking from time to time after the whereabouts of the Mission of San Miguel – where he had heard that Father Soler had a cure for warts – but, while he found the folk pleasant and willing to help where they could, frustration crept into the affair, for nobody had heard of the mission he sought, and he was assured by those who had the best reason to know – those, indeed, who had lived in these parts all their lives – that he had been misinformed. And so

it went from disconcerting to disappointing, and a
depressed Oak was inclining to the belief that he
had come south on a fool's errand when, at almost
midnight, he climbed onto his horse again and
rode out on the moonwashed road that led to Old
Mexico, wilfully set on making his bed still
further south. Stubborn rather than faithful, he
was now determined – to the point of perversity
itself – not to give up the dream that Santa Rita
seemed to have decried. He would get word of San
Miguel somewhere. That mission was there, and
he would find it somehow.

He arose from his blankets next morning stiff
and jaded. It had been well into the early hours
when the setting moon had shown him this corner
beside a mountain stream and he had settled
down to sleep. All the inspiration had gone out of
him now, the voice of his romantic determination
was muted, and his belief in sudden riches and
good years had become threadbare. He had kept
going too long – driven himself too hard. Fatigue
had different effects on different people, and he
reckoned that last night he must have been drunk
on it. Drunk on alcohol he most certainly had not
been, for small beer stimulated the kidneys and
very little else. Was he, then, to face round and go
home? Now there was a laugh! He had no home to
go to, and Coopville would certainly be the death
of him. That was if he didn't get planted after a
little bit of trouble on the way there. No, he'd go
forward – if only on account of having nothing else
to do – and maybe at the limit of his mount's

strength and his own patience, he'd find himself a job. If he could put two hundred dollars together, he might buy a few woollies and go into sheepherding. It had always struck him as a nice restful sort of job and, as he was no natural-born cowman, he could stand the smell of sheep and eat mutton as often as he had to. He'd think some more about it.

He had a wash and put a razor to his face. Then he ate a hunch of bread and drank some water from his washed out and newly filled canteen. All the time his eyes roved over the scene about him. There were ridges and cliffs everywhere, rising to peaks and scudding vapours, and glimpses of forest too and the odd cascade, with the air tremulous and birdsong coming out of the woods at his back. Red baneberry flashed at him, new to the sun, and pink and purple asters grew about a log that was black and white with rot. The fragrance of the opening flowers flavoured the morning. It was beautiful, but it was wild too. Wild and forbidding, and he was reminded that the natural world simply existed. Man used it as a stage, and if he had no purpose to work upon it he should not be there. He was an intruder at the best of times.

Oak swallowed the last of his bread. Then he shook out and rolled up his blankets. After that, burdened of either hand, he walked over to where his horse was grazing. He looped his canteen back to the pommel, then tied his blanketroll behind the cantle. Now he swung back into his saddle

and, regaining what trail there was, headed down
country to the right of the rising sun. As if in proof –
if he needed it – that men had passed this way
before him, he came upon intersecting trails at
intervals, and some had been signposted. Hurley,
Hatch, Silver City – Central; none seemed all that
far away. And even Lordsberg was no great distance from here. This empty land must in fact be
crawling with humankind. Yet he seemed to have
the planet to himself, and was damned if he could
give it away. Now there was a bargain for somebody. Just give him San Miguel, and the other guy
could have the rest.

Smiling bleakly to himself, Oak reflected that he
had truly got the megrims this morning; but then
he heard voices up front – one in particular, male
and strident, and a woman's too, ringing and
fearful – and the gloom lifted instantly from his
mind. Easing back on his reins, he closed slowly on
the corner before him that concealed whatever the
noise was about; and, rounding it with the greatest
caution, saw a body of horsemen making the final
preparations to hang a young man and a girl with
dark good looks from the bough of a trailside wild
cherry tree.

The pair, hands bound behind them, already sat
their mounts beneath the branch, and the hang-
ropes had just been tightened around their necks.
Now the majority of the men present were retreat-
ing, but one bulky figure, afoot and dressed in
riding britches and a cord jacket, was standing
directly behind the horses supporting the condem-

ned couple with a whip raised.

Oak didn't think about it. He jerked and cocked his revolver. Rough justice he could not abide. Too often it was an expediency and no justice at all. 'Hold it, you callous sidewinders!' he yelled, firing a shot at the whip that the well-dressed executioner was about to bring down on the rump of the young man's horse; and he hit his target, plucking the whip out of the heavy man's grasp.

The would-be executioner gaped in Oak's direction for a long moment, then went for the gun on his right hip. Oak promptly shot the other through the forearm. Crying out, the man turned aside and stood holding his wound, blood spilling through his fingers. 'Anybody else?' Oak called. 'I'd hate to close the bidding with somebody left unsatisfied.'

It was plain that the members of the lynch party had seen enough. There were no more foolish movements. 'I congratulate you, gents,' Oak now approved, indicating a middle-aged man in a work-blue shirt and battered grey Stetson with a twitch of his gun barrel. 'You. Go and free them.'

The man nodded. 'I have to take a knife out.'

'Do it,' Oak said. 'Funny stuff will get you a bullet.'

The man in the battered hat fished out a shut-knife and opened the big blade. Then he left his companions – the majority of whom remained mounted – and walked over to where the young fellow and the dark girl still sat their mounts somewhat precariously under the cherry bough. Reaching up behind the girl, the man with the knife quickly severed the bindings on her wrists, and she just as swiftly lifted her freed hands and threw the noose off her neck, looking enormously relieved. After that the blade did its work on her companion's bonds, and he too removed the halter from his throat in double quick time.

'I thank you,' Oak called to the man in the battered grey Stetson. 'Now come back here.'

The other moved to obey, putting up his shut-knife.

'I want the rest of you who're still mounted to climb down,' Oak barked. 'Hurry it! Now run off your horses! All of you!'

There was a half-hearted yipping and yelling, and a beating at equine rumps with hand and hat. The horses went galloping off in all directions, leaving their ten or a dozen owners to gaze after them with faces that registered expressions from rage to dismay.

'Nicely,' Oak once more approved. 'Gunbelts next, if you please. Take 'em off, and cast them as far as you can behind the hanging tree.'

Again he was obeyed, though the young fellow and the girl whom he had just rescued helped themselves to a pistol each from among the men present before the gunbelts were hurled away.

'Fine,' Oak said laconically. 'Now I want you all to know this. I have an objection to being followed. I shoot at people who come after me, and I don't often miss. There's been little harm done, so I suggest you all go home when you've rounded up your property and forget what's happened here. That way we may all grow old and die in our beds. Okay?'

No response came, either negative or positive – but then he hadn't really expected any – and, raising the muzzle of his pistol to his temple in mocking salute, he spurred his horse straight at the figures loosely assembled before him. They scattered all ways, and he carried on down the trail, throwing back a single glance at the two young people whom he had lately saved from death, leaving them to follow him or not as they saw fit.

He covered about two miles before craning again, and was not too surprised to see the pair galloping along less than a hundred yards behind him. Well, he wasn't about to pull up – it was still too close to the action for that – but he did feel, now the miles of tree-covered space had opened up on his right, a departure from the beaten track was in order, and he drew off to the west, again leaving it to the pair at his back to either continue following him or suit their own devices.

Riding the more open ways of the forest when he could, Oak went on for another half an hour; then, seeing that his mount had lathered up and was starting to suffer, he showed respect for its years and drew rein beside a moss-clad rockpile, bracing himself off one of the upper stones and letting his jaw sag over his outstretched left arm. He didn't look back, but heard hoofbeats coming up fast, and a few moments later the rescued pair halted beside him. 'Hello,' he greeted, adding a smile and a jerky little nod as he slanted his gaze at them.

'Hi,' the young man responded. 'Thanks.'

'You're welcome.'

'You took a big risk for us,' the girl said, hazel-eyed under her black curls, pale skinned, and exquisitely chiselled around the mouth and nostrils. 'We're truly grateful.'

'I had the drop,' Oak reminded, 'and that fool who went for his gun gave me the chance to show what I could do.' He smiled again. 'But I have to ask it. Were you guilty or innocent?'

At once merry-eyed and rueful, the young man gave it a moment's thought, then said wryly: 'Guilty.'

'Enough to swing for?'

'Twenty dollars out of the storekeeper's till?'

'I wouldn't say,' Oak said. 'I'm Bob Oak.'

'Stokes – Jed and Sally.'

'Husband and wife?'

'No, we're brother and sister.'

Oak considered the other's strongly built and middle-sized person. He could see the resemblance now, but imagined it was a case of the boy favouring his mother and the girl her father. 'D'you go in for helping yourselves?'

'It's a bad habit we've got into.'

'It is a bad habit, Jed,' Oak said seriously. 'I had it myself one time. You never rest easy, and it gets you into bad company.'

'We're not proud of it, Mr Oak,' the girl said. 'It started while pa was still alive. A varmint of a cattle baron, Nicolas Dumont – the man you shot through the arm back there – threw us off our farm, and we had to make shift. We intended to make it just one robbery at the start, and we held up a stagecoach. We picked up two hundred dollars on that job, but money is soon spent, and it leaves you with the need for more.'

'So you robbed another stage,' Oak prompted.

'No, a tax collector.'

'You're moving on.'

'And then a bank.'

'You're getting educated.'

'We even tried a train,' the girl said, laughing a little shyly.

'That's graduation,' Oak acknowledged. 'You're a desperate couple.'

'I don't know,' Jed Stokes doubted. 'Sally would rather get married, and I like watching my crops grow. Outlawry isn't what it's cracked up to be, and it takes you round the same old circle.'

'When it doesn't take you to prison or the cemetery,' Oak said significantly.

'I guess we never figured we'd get caught, Bob.'

'There's a law of averages, Jed,' Oak reminded. 'We're all subject to it. Did those skunks get you after a chase?'

'From Presterville,' Sally Stokes put in. 'That's a small town a few miles from here. Home ground for us. We figured we'd got the routine at the store weighed to an ounce. We had too; but that didn't stop everything going wrong. We should have stayed away from Bruce Renton's store.'

'Needs must sometimes,' Oak reflected. 'How did your pa die?'

'Of a cough,' Jed replied. 'The doctor called it consumption. But we thnk he pined to death for ma.'

'Saw something of the kind in my own family,' Oak said. 'Only it was the other way round. Doc said ma had a bad heart. But I knew she had a broken one. And I didn't help much.'

'Seems we're three of a kind,' the girl observed.

'I don't reckon the world would miss us much at that,' Oak growled. 'But it's up to us to stay alive as long as we can. Are we safe here, Jed?'

'No.'

'They'll give chase?'

'Nick Dumont will,' Jed Stokes said. 'His Circle D has the resources. He won't forgive that shot arm in a hurry.'

'Sounds like I ought to have plugged him dead centre,' Oak commented grimly.

'You're no killer, Mr Oak!' the girl protested.

Oak was touched by her warm defence of what she couldn't know; but he cleared his throat and considered it would be unwise to go any further into it just then.

'We have a first class hideout,' Stokes said. 'You can come there with us if you like.'

'Where – and how far?'

'It matters to you, Bob?'

'Yes.'

'South – and ten miles.'

Sally Stokes said. 'It's a cave in a high and lonely place. We found it by chance. A mountain man died there years ago. We buried his bones.' There was amusement in her eyes. 'You're not afraid of ghosts?'

'Yes,' Oak said bluntly. 'Though I'm not expecting to meet any.'

'You were headed someplace,' Ted asked perci-piently, 'when you broke off to do us a hand's turn?'

Oak nodded.

Jed's lifting eyebrows questioned.

Oak shook his head. He'd run across a dubious couple here; and, though he had no bad feelings about them – and even felt an instinctive trust and liking towards them – he didn't wish to throw any strain upon the more acquisitive aspects of their natures by arousing their suspicions as to his reason for being in these parts.

'If there's anything we can do to help you,' Jed said, 'you've only to ask.'

The gravity in Stokes' eyes did it. For all the evidence to the contrary, Oak felt that he was looking into the soul of an honest man. He thought he'd chance it after all. These two undoubtedly got around, and if there was a San Miguel, they were more likely to have heard of it than almost anybody else. 'I'm looking for a certain Spanish mission,' he said. 'I talked to some folk back in Santa Rita, and they seemed to think it didn't exist. Have you ever heard of San Miguel?'

'Sure.'

Oak looked at the ground. 'Ah! And there's a mission there?'

'No.'

Oak could have hit the guy, but he controlled himself. That was how people let you down. It seemed like one more disappointment to put with the rest.

Seven

Looking towards Sally Stokes, Oak perceived her anxious, half-pleading expression and had a strong feeling that he had misunderstood her brother. 'What is it?'

'There isn't now,' the girl explained. 'There was once.'

'That's right,' Jed Stokes resumed. 'A big piece of a cliff came down on the mission and covered it up. It happened during the great storms of Eighteen twenty. Or that's how I heard it. Nearby the ruins of the village remain. One old man still lives there.'

'Long may he do so,' Oak said resignedly. 'That's that then.'

'What was so important to you there?' Sally asked.

Feeling cheated and aggrieved – and generally depressed to boot – Oak took the treasure map from his pocket and, convinced that his secret no longer mattered, handed it to the girl. Sally began studying it uncomprehendingly, and he started telling its story; then, as understanding dawned, the girl passed it to her brother, who heard Oak

93

out while looking at it and then said: 'I've heard some tales of Aztec treasure in my time, but that one's the match of any. The cup was surely dashed from your lips, Bob. It's enough to make the angels weep!'

Oak took back the small piece of vellum and returned it to his pocket. 'I suppose I was never really certain of it. There was always a doubt. I had the feeling that it couldn't be real.'

'The dream was real,' the girl said sympathetically. 'It isn't as if the place wasn't there – once.'

'The remains of the mission are still there,' Jed Stokes said thoughtfully. 'Yes, they're buried under tons of earth and rock; but, if there was a treasure, it must still be down there with them.'

'But buried far too deep to get at,' Oak mused in his turn.

'We don't know for that,' Stokes said. 'Landslides leave uneven spreads of rubble behind them. Nobody has ever had cause to closely examine what happened at San Miguel. Wouldn't do any harm if we paid the place a visit and had a look round the slide. We might as well go to San Miguel as anywhere. This isn't a district we're going to be safe in for months to come.'

'If ever again,' Sally Stokes remarked gloomily. 'You know how Nicolas Dumont feels about me.'

'Eh?' Oak inquired quickly. 'He looked to be getting past all that.'

'Old bulls are the worst,' Jed Stokes commented. 'Dumont ran us off our farm as much because Sally cold-shouldered him as because he wanted the land.'

'Yet he was going to lynch her.'

'The same as having her once for all in his wicked old nature,' Stokes responded. 'Yes, it shocks, man, but that's the size of it.'

'There's plenty in human nature that shocks,' Oak acknowledged. 'Well, if I don't go to San Miguel now, it figures you two will. So I think I'd better go along. No harm in seeing the place, and that's a fact.'

'We ought to get moving again,' Sally Stokes said, craning to her rear and shivering. 'If that bunch from Presterville did ride after us as soon as they'd got their horses and guns backs, they needn't be too far behind. Tracking us through the forest would be no great feat.'

'We'll ride up to the hideout,' her brother said decisively. 'It's pretty much on our way anyhow. We can eat up there and rest awhile. The moon is still at its best for night travel. We can carry on after dark if you like, Bob.'

'Fine by me,' Oak replied.

'It's about twenty miles from the hideout,' the girl said. 'A bit left of the line between Silver City and Lordsberg.'

'I guess the map doesn't show it too accurately,' Oak said. 'Off you go, Jed!'

Stokes fetched round, and led off between south and west. Presently they entered the thickest of the forest around, and rode through dense shadows and heavy airs, the sudden slashes of sunlight through the tall timber burning like heated swords and the gnats jigging their death dance under the lower boughs. All the time Oak and company were climbing somewhat; and then they came to terraced rock and truly ascended, the air getting cooler and the aspens about them streaming a million tiny points of light down the breeze off the high passes. They toiled on and upwards, and it wasn't long before they approached the upper limit of the treeline, where they followed a grey wall westwards for a mile or so before turning a sharp corner of rock onto a wide ledge that inclined outwards and slightly up from the mouth of a large cave that was framed in wet mildew and looked northwards out of eternal shadow. 'Home sweet home,' Stokes said ironically. 'Don't forget to wipe your feet.'

Oak grinned despite himself, and the three of them dismounted and ground-tied their horses in a rocky bay to the right of the cavern. 'There's a mountain meadow below and to the west of us,' Sally Stokes said. 'We graze the animals down there, and that's also where we buried the remains of the first tenant. Game's abundant, and there's a place to fish too.'

'Not quite all the conveniences,' Jed Stokes added.

'You look well on it anyhow,' Oak confided.

They entered the cave. It smelled faintly of cooking fires, and the ceiling was thick with soot. Pulp sacks filled with hay provided two beds, an oaken bucket contained the water supply, and stockfish and strips of jerked beef hung from a

line across the rear corner of the place on the left.
Two fruit boxes formed the only seating present,
and some tin utensils stood on a white hand towel.
It was all primitive in the last degree – and must
be subject to bitter cold during the winter days –
but it was sanctuary enough for two young people
who would at least lose their freedom if they
showed their faces where the law-abiding kept the
fleshpots.

Stokes built a fire, and his sister selected some
meat to boil in a pot of wild onions. Still having
bread left in his saddlebag, Oak supplied a loaf for
the meal – something that his companions seemed
to regard as a luxury – then walked to the front of
the ledge that abutted the cave and looked out
across the slopes and timbertops below, seeking
any signs of pursuit. He did not expect to see any,
and went to his vigil somewhat casually because
of it, so he received the shock he deserved when,
off to the southeast – and well beyond the height
at which the sharp angle of stone at the start of
the ledge cut off all view of the route which he and
the two other fugitives had used to get here – he
made out a party of horsemen riding the grasses
that thinned into the trees along the forest's edge,
minute figures peering this way and that in their
obvious uncertainty.

It was the men from Presterville all right, and
he could see that well-dressed man was ramrod-
ding them. Perhaps that arm wound he had given
the fellow hadn't been as serious as the bleeding
had made it look. Again he found it in him to wish

that he had shot Dumont in the chest. For he'd
swear that, without the big rancher's will behind
them, the townsmen would have heeded his
warning and gone home. After all, he had told
them the truth – no great harm had been done –
and it was madness how a stymied act of rough
justice was now building up into a hunt that could
result in a good many deaths.

Turning away from the vantage, Oak walked
back into the cave and told the other two what he
had seen. Both paled; then, by tacit agreement,
the three of them strode to the spot which Oak
had occupied at the outer edge of shelf and gazed
down and away to the right, shielding their eyes
from the glare of the sun as they watched their
hunters now heading back into the forest with the
apparent intention of withdrawing from the area.
'I couldn't see Indian Charlie among them, Jed,'
Sally said to her brother as the last of the
horsemen vanished into the trees. 'Did you see
him?'

'No,' Jed Stokes said abstractedly. 'No, I didn't
see him.'

'He would have been in front, wouldn't he?'

'That's the place you'd expect, Sally – sure.'

'What is this?' Oak inquired, a trifle irritated.
'Am I supposed to know?'

'They had Indian Charlie Betts with them,' the
girl explained. 'I saw Charlie there when they
were putting the noose over my head. He's the
best tracker for a hundred miles. You can be sure
it was him brought them this far.'

'They've never been this close before,' Stokes said tensely.

'They've never been anywhere near us before,' the girl corrected.

'Don't start panicking,' Oak said in a voice that was cold and firm. 'They're still plenty far from finding you yet.'

'Folk have the habit of returning to a likely spot,' Jed reminded.

'Can't deny that,' Oak said.

Jed sighed heavily.

'I wish I'd spotted Indian Charlie,' the girl muttered.

Her brother turned his head towards the cave. 'What's that hissing noise? Your cooking pot must have tipped, Sal.'

'Oh, dear!' Sally exclaimed in annoyance; and she faced about and ran back into the cave.

'I daresay I'll have to relight that damned fire,' Stokes said. 'Are you going to keep watch out here a bit longer, Bob?'

'You can call me when the food is ready,' Oak said, nodding.

Eyes looking down, Jed walked off in the direction that his sister had already taken.

Oak gazed across the country about him. It was vast in span, largely enclosed by peaks, and full of light. A new wind was in the trees below, sweeping the green foliage, and he could hear a chinking of fragments where draughts from the same source scoured dusty corners of the naked stone formations above the cave. The blustering

cool brought an invigorating quality with it, and
Oak turned slow circles to extract the best from
the currents that whisked about him – this
exercise altering his outlook often enough to make
him aware of the tiniest changes in the scene
below – and all at once he glimpsed a coyote's
sudden dive, rabbit in mouth, away from the foot
of a shrub, and wondered at it, for the creature
had been perfectly hidden and must have been
badly startled to have exposed itself thus.

Then Oak saw a moving feather at the further
side of the shrub, and the top of the hat that bore
it appeared a moment later. After that a
copper-skinned man in a black skirt and pants
came into view, conchos glinting on his loose
waistcoat. The fellow was undoubtedly a half
breed, and unquestionably Indian Charlie. His
tan pony was climbing on sure hooves, and the
man himself was the picture of watchful
concentration.

Oak centred all his attention on the other. No
wonder Sally Stokes hadn't seen Indian Charlie
among the Presterville horsemen. The man had
been no longer with the party. He must have
detached himself minutes before and already been
on his way up here when Oak had first spotted the
riders who had recently re-entered the forest. It
figured that Charlie, redskin stubborn, had
wanted to continue the search that his companions had been ready to abandon. Damn the
half breed for the brutish excellence of his
instincts! He was too gifted for his own good!

Oak watched the other with growing anxiety. The guy was already well towards the treeline. Hopefully he would turn back down before long. From his present position – unless he had prior knowledge of the cave's existence – he could not possibly suspect that it was there, and bare rock as a rule offered few attractions to the man seeking at hazard. But Indian Charlie seemed to lack that kind of sensitivity to his surroundings. He kept coming and, as he neared the limit of the aspens, the watching Oak lost all hope that he would turn back of his own accord.

There seemed nothing for it. The man would have to be confronted. Short of killing him, there was little to do but rob him of his gun and set him afoot. It would take him the rest of the day to walk home to Presterville – which meant that the fugitives would have ample time to quit the cave and put many a mile between them and a resumed pursuit – but it also meant that their refuge on this high lonesome would be lost to them from this day forth. Knowing what the right kind of shelter meant to those on the dodge, Oak felt more sympathy for Jed and Sally Stokes on that issue than anything, and he cudgelled his brains for some solution that would leave blood unspilled and the secret of the cave's presence intact. But there was clearly no answer to the problem except in what was already obvious, and he resigned himself to simply doing the best he could when the time arrived.

Deciding not to worry Jed and Sally with the

problem, Oak eased his gun in leather and headed for the end of the shelf on his right. Rounding the massive prow of granite at that point, he kept back in the shadows and looked down towards the tree-line. Indian Charlie was now well into the rock-lands and climbing directly towards him. Filled with the idea of heading the other off somewhat, Oak crouched low and glided into the descent, using the largest of the boulders around to hide him; but even so he must have shown something of himself in his approach work, for Indian Charlie Betts suddenly called: 'Stop creepin' about, you damned fool, and stand up like a man!'

Less chagrined than shamed by the contempt in the half breed's voice, Oak stepped into the open and drew himself fully erect. 'I can do that, Charlie,' he said.

'Oh,' responded the half breed, grinning humourlessly at the use of his name, 'you've still got that Stokes pair with you. Birds of a feather, eh?'

'You're the one who sprouts feathers,' Oak replied, totally watchful despite his apparent negligence.

'You comin' back with me, feller, peaceable like?'

'You must be off your rocker, Charlie.'

'Presents a problem, don't it?'

'Easily solved.'

'Ow?'

'Jump off your nag, feller, and throw your gun away.'

'I'm tired o' throwing my gun away,' Indian

Charlie retorted. 'I've done that once today already.'

'And you're a man who gets easily bored.'

'You could say that.'

'I know how it is,' Oak admitted. 'But it's that or get hurt.'

'You hurt me?' Charlie queried, face alight with mockery as he shook his head and added: 'No – no – no.'

'I've done talking.'

The half breed swung out of his saddle, then stepped clear of his horse. 'So start shooting.'

Oak knew himself to have a faster gun than most. He hoped to be able to plug his adversary through the right arm or shoulder before Indian Charlie could get into action. The shock of stopping a forty-four slug in the moving parts that mattered should preclude further shooting. But Oak had no sooner gone to the draw than he realized that the other was as fast as he. Thus he was only too glad to let his hammer fall in the split second that his revolver levelled. Indian Charlie's gun flashed simultaneously, and his bullet clipped the collar of Oak's shirt as the half breed twisted away and fell on his face. Knowing the worst, Oak holstered his pistol and walked slowly over to the inert figure. Putting a toe under the half breed's chest, he turned Charlie onto his back, and the copper-skinned man stared up at him with newly-dead eyes. It was the strange innocence in that dark gaze which made the victor spit.

Oak turned away. Practically speaking, there was nothing to be done but leave the corpse lying and the horse standing. Body and brute weren't going to betray anything up here – though the horsemen from Presterville could still be close enough to have heard the shots and to have placed them better than approximately. Blasted guns kicked up such a row! He had been planning to jump that consarned breed as quietly as possible, but how often did a plan turn out as intended?

Looking up, Oak slanted back in the direction of the great cornerstone above, and just then Jed and Sally Stokes rounded the mass and peered down towards him. 'What's happened, Bob?' Sally called, her eyes flicking on and off the nearby body in the most apprehensive of manners. 'Is that Indian Charlie?'

'It's no good blaming me,' Oak snapped at her, reading the accusation in her brother's stare.

'You've surely gone and done it,' Jed Stokes observed.

'It was his choice,' Oak said shortly. 'There was no way I could get out of it, short of shooting my gun. It was him or me.'

'That puts us into the real Wanted list,' Jed said, pulling an ear.

Oak joined them at the high corner. 'What do you expect? I told you you'd graduated.'

'It's our fault,' Sally said decisively. 'None of this would have happened if we hadn't tried to rob that store on home territory.'

'There's the truth, boy,' Oak said flatly. 'Let's

pull ourselves together. You did nothing. I've got
to live with it. Now there's a strong chance those
shots were heard by the riders from Presterville.
They can't be more than a few miles from here. If
they come back, they'll find the body – and they'll
likely search further then – so we'd better be long
gone.'

'I knew when the pot spilled we weren't going to
get that meal,' Sally said resentfully.

'You're not the first woman to see her cooking
wasted,' Oak comforted – or otherwise – beck-
oning as he moved off round the prow of granite.

Regaining the ledge, he crossed the mouth of
the cave and led into the bay where the horses
were secured. Freeing the brutes of their
ground-ties was the work of a moment, and
backing the mounts out onto the broad stone
apron took hardly longer. They got ready to leave
the hideout, but Oak indicated that they ought to
put the cooking fire out first. Sally went into the
cave and extinguished the flames by tipping the
contents of her pot over them, while the two men
outside grimaced at each other in hungry regret
over their loss as clouds of smoky steam that were
redolent of the dinner table wafted to their
nostrils.

They left the jutting shelf with their horses on
lead, but returned to their saddles at the top of the
slope beyond. As they went forward again, Oak
reminded them that San Miguel was their goal.
Now Jed Stokes took over the lead. Ignoring the
corpse and the horse that still drooped near it,

they descended to the point that their leader required, then broke sharply to the left, crossing the upper line of the aspens. After that they followed sunken narrows floored with bunch-grass, a low black wall on their left, and emerged onto what Oak knew must be the mountain meadow which Sally had mentioned.

Here they descended what amounted to a fine mingling of grass, mosses, and erica. Turkeys were plentiful, as were quail and red deer, and loping jack-rabbits showed the way into the dark world of the ponderosa pines, where the surfaced roots were massive, the ferns half as high as a man, and the resin-charged humidity so great that it was difficult to breathe. But the cathedral gloom of the huge vaults under the boughs soon opened into the sunlight again, and Oak and company began to traverse declining rocklands which merged with the flats on the western side of the Black Range where purple sage and greasewood grew in abundance.

Their course slipped southwards. Eventually they approached a cliff which buttressed the western flank of a minor peak. Aware from the lie of the land that they must soon join the flats, Oak looked forward to a spell of easier riding after the ceaseless care which crossing the high ground had enforced, and he was starting to relax his cramped groin and hip muscles, when a small, circular light struck the surface of the cliff ahead and literally flashed across it, vanishing almost as soon as it had come.

Tensed up again, and slightly lifted out of leather, Oak waited for this curious phenomenon to reappear – conscious that his companions had missed it completely – but the light did not reoccur and Oak could only crane upwards and back, seeking for its source with straining eyes, but there was no movement of any kind upon the heights to the east of them.

Oak settled back into his saddle. That flying light had not occurred naturally. There had been a human agency behind it. That circle of brightness had been a reflection cast from far off. Somebody had picked up the sun for an instant before closing the end of a telescope with his eye. He and the Stokes pair were being spied on. By a watcher from the Presterville party? It was just about possible, though Dumont and his followers would have had to cover ground at a pretty remarkable rate to have reached a relatively nearby vantage point so quickly.

Pondering it time and again, Oak found himself almost wanting to believe that he and his companions were being overlooked by Dumont and company, but he could not quite credit it. There was somebody else up there.

Pete Brett? It could be. He had more or less forgotten the man in the pressure of more recent events. If it were Brett up there, the complications were coming fast. How was it all going to end? And where?

Eight

They were several miles further down country from where Oak had seen the flying disc of radiance when he decided that he would have to tell his companions the whole of his personal story – at least in so far as Coopville and his troubles there had been concerned – since he could hardly expect them to react well if matters should suddenly come to a head and they hadn't the first idea of what it was all about. They also had the right to part from him at the earliest moment if they so wished, for there could be no question that he was a dangerous man to be around, and they had problems enough without the additional ones that his immediate past could throw up.

So, making it plain from the start that what he had to impart was very serious and they should listen extra carefully, Oak spoke first of what he had seen back at the cliff, telling then of Pete Brett and his fears arising from the man. Then he went back to his release from the Denver prison and his visit to Uncle George's home in Coopville – this leading into the events which had occurred

there and passing into all the rest of it, including
Heidi's part, culminating in his wild escape from
Coopville and the ride down the valley of the Rio
Grande which had brought about his meeting
with them. 'It's not an easy story to follow,' he
reflected at the last, 'but I've given you all the
facts. I wouldn't have told you any of it – for my
own pride's sake – if I hadn't just now felt obliged
to. My aim was to give you choice. You don't have
to stick around me. If you feel it's in your own best
interests to go your own way, go now. We're not
sixty miles from Arizona. Plenty of new trails to
ride, and places to hide in, over there.'

'If it hadn't been for you, Bob,' Jed Stokes said
soberly, 'Sally and I would be dead and buried by
now. I said if we could help you in any way, we'd
give that help.' He glanced at his sister. 'Yes?'

'Yes,' she replied emphatically.

'It looks to me as if you need help about now,
Bob.'

'Numbers make strength,' Oak admitted. 'But I
set out alone, and I reckon I can finish alone. No
sense dragging you two down with me.'

'Do you prefer to go on alone?'

'I didn't say that,' Oak responded. 'The choice is
entirely yours; you are free to please yourself. I
reckon you'd be safer shut of me – especially as it
figures we shall have to split up sooner or later.'

'No hard feelings?'

'Hell, no, Jed!'

'Sally?' her brother asked.

'I vote we stick together.'

'So do I,' Jed Stokes said.

'That's jake with me,' Oak confided. 'I only hope you don't have cause to regret it.'

'The regret will be ours only.'

'Mine too,' Oak said heavily. 'I'd like to see you two living straight lives. Neither one of you fits the criminal bill.'

'You do?' Sally asked.

'Trouble finds me,' Oak said shortly.

'Perhaps you invite it,' the girl hazarded.

'Maybe he needs it,' Jed laughed. 'He sure can handle it.'

'What gifts I have,' Oak said in a bored voice, 'a man is better off without. Now let's leave it alone.'

His words were plain, and his will accepted. He knew in himself that he had been recognised as the natural leader, and he felt a certain responsibility because of it. These two were able people, but their hearts weren't really in what they were doing, and they needed to follow his firmer lines of thought. Not to put too fine a point on it, they felt a strength in him that they believed they lacked. It was flattering, but it was also burdensome. He had supposed at first that the faint possibility of wealth at San Miguel had been their motivation for standing by him; but now he perceived that neither that nor gratitude had much to do with it. They simply needed him and, if he had not liked them both, he would have felt inclined to ignore any advantage which they might represent to himself and shake them off. If only because he was made like that and operated a loner's charter.

They rode on in silence. Now three pairs of eyes
scanned their back-trail and the heights on their
left with increased intentness. Yet Oak had no
instinctive awareness of being closely pursued,
and his tension soon ebbed because of it. As a
natural reaction, he began to wonder whether he
had deceived himself in the matter of the flying
light, but he realized that the chance of his having
made any mistake was fairly remote, and he
forced himself to accept that he was dealing with
a patient hunter who was sufficiently primed to
swoop in only at the moment of greatest
advantage. It was Pete Brett all right, and he was
now convinced that the man had been there or
thereabouts from the beginning. That old mental
affinity – the lodestone of like badness between
two similar minds – was now drawing them with
an ever more powerful certainty towards the
showdown which Oak feared. This fatal consciousness made him more withdrawn and un-
communicative than ever.

The horses slowed, and the miles extended. The
day began to fade. Oak could see the weakness of
their situation, and hoped for rock to cross, but
their route seemed to take them over unending
fields of sand and loose grit. Behind them their
tracks were all too visible to the naked eye. Then,
as the eastern skyline faded and the west rioted
with the splash and gleam of a fiery afterglow, the
underfoot changed into broad outcrops of granitic
stone. Now Jed Stokes made an abrupt change of
direction, heading nearer west than south and

remarking that things had come about much as he wished. 'The dusk is hiding our turn,' he explained, 'and anybody who seeks our tracks here in tomorrow's light will find nothing. We shall lay down little further sign between this spot and San Miguel.'

'We're about eight miles short,' Sally said.

'Let's get there as quickly as we can,' Oak returned. 'I know the horses are tuckered out, but we can't help that. It's the spy-glass that we mustn't forget. If we're off the land tomorrow morning, there'll be nothing for an enemy to climb high and look for.'

'That's good thinking,' Jed Stokes commented. 'San Miguel lies low anyhow. It's a place you'd miss more times than not if you didn't know it was there. As I told you, only the ruins of the village remain, with one old man still living there. I reckon we could find safe haven in that place.'

'If it works out like that – fine,' Oak said; but he thought it unlikely and his voice betrayed the fact. 'Do you know the old man's name, Sally?'

'Emilio Cruz,' the girl answered.

'Figure he'll sell us some grub?' Oak inquired. 'We can't keep going on wind.'

'I doubt he's got much, Bob,' Jed Stokes said. 'There's water there, and some grass, so the horses will be able to feed.'

'Their bellies are more important than ours,' Oak agreed. 'I have a bit of grub left in my bags, but we shan't get fat on what there is.'

Again they rode in silence. Rock piled at them

now. Great buttes stood black and just visible
behind the bar of smoky gold that lighted the
middle distance. Metallic echoes marked the
passing of their mounts, and a star trembled in
the purple dome of the midheaven, while a
glimmer of the lurking moon told of mists off to
their left. Oak suffered the illusion that they were
covering the same piece of ground over and over
again. But they were moving forward, and
eventually this became plain, for a considerable
crest reared into the low starlight of the south.
The summit appeared to be the highest point in
an arc of cliffs that formed the back of an
extensive low into which the presently declining
earth was bearing them and, judging from the
time factor and the clues previously given, Oak
thought they must be nearing journey's end. 'This
it, Jed?' he asked.

'San Miguel, yes,' Stokes replied.

Then, still some distance ahead of them, a dog
started barking. It appeared the animal had
either heard or sensed their approach and wanted
it known to the limits of the night that strangers
were around. Nor did the brute let up. Its yapping
went on incessantly – growing louder by the
moment as the slope brought them nearer to the
source – and Oak felt that this Emilio Cruz,
assuming the dog did belong to him, must be a
remarkably patient man. For Oak feared that,
had the animal been his, he'd long ago have done
it a mischief had it kept up such a loud baying for
minutes on end.

'I believe that dog is trying to tell us something,' Sally Stokes said, as they reached the bottom of the slope and began to cross the lower ground beyond.

'Like what?' Oak inquired.

'I think it's suffering,' the girl said uncertainly.

Oak listened more carefully, and detected a wailing note amidst the yapping. The girl could be right. 'We'd better go and see,' he said.

They homed in on the barking, traversing land that was perfectly flat, free from all rock debris – if choked with weeds and cacti – and gave the impression of having once been fields in which men had toiled for generations. Clearing this ground, and drawing closer to the western end of the arc of cliffs, they came upon adobe ruins in the light of the just risen moon, and before long they approached a structure that Oak perceived to be a complete home.

A shape stirred on the dwelling's front step. Jet black and green eyed, it was unquestionably the dog. Now the brute stopped barking, thumped its tail on the slab of stone, then threw back its head and let out a dreadful howl. 'I don't like this!' Sally declared. 'There's something wrong here!'

Reining in, Oak swung stiffly to the ground. 'I'll have a look inside. You two wait out here.'

Thumbs hooked into his gunbelt, Oak sauntered up to the front door of the house. He was extremely watchful, since he feared what the dog might do in the first instance; but, short of attacking him, it licked his right hand and appeared to feel that its duty was done. After that it walked off to Oak's left and disappeared round the corner in that direction towards the rear of the house.

Oak halted on the doorstep. He saw that the door itself stood open, and that the room beyond was in darkness. Putting his head round the jamb, he knocked on the woodwork, 'Anybody at home?' he asked. 'Senor Cruz?'

There was no answer. Taking out a match, he stepped into the house, ripping fire on his canvas seat. Then he held up the flame, letting what radiance it had to offer pulse about the room. Some of the light fell back upon a table at the middle of the sanded floor, and Oak saw an oil lamp standing on the cotton centre-piece. Walking to the lamp, he touched off the wick; then, after shaking out his match and making a small adjustment to the light, he lifted the lamp high and let its rays slant into the four corners of the room.

The glow touched a bed which stood back from the moon-washed window on his left. He made out a thin face on the pillow under the head-rail. Taking three quick paces towards the bed, Oak leaned forward, holding his lamp close to the face adjacent and studying it intently. The jaw had fallen, the sinuses were sunken and tallowy, and the glazed eyes went on staring dully as he passed a hand above them. There was a faint smell of corruption present too, and that more than anything confirmed what had happened. The man on the bed had died – perhaps three or four days ago – and the noisy behaviour of the dog was thus explained. 'Jed – Sally!' Oak called over his left shoulder. 'Will you come in here, please?'

He heard the pair jump down from their horses, and they entered the house a few moments later and hurried across the room to join him. Standing one at his either shoulder, they gazed down on the bed in the light from his still lowered lamp. 'I'm afraid he's dead as a doornail,' Oak said. 'That is Emilio Cruz?'

'Yes,' the girl replied, 'that's Emilio.'

Jed blew softly through his lips. 'He needs burying.'

'Without much delay,' Oak agreed.

'I wonder what came to him?' Sally mused.

'I don't aim to examine the body,' Oak said. 'I can't see any signs of violence, and there are no obvious traces of disease. By the look of him, I'd say Emilio must have been pretty old; so I'll be content to put his death down to old age.'

'There's a candlestick on the mantelpiece,' Jed observed. 'I reckon I'll light me a light, then go into the back room and see if I can find a shovel.'

'I'm going to prepare this poor old body for burial in a proper manner,' Sally announced. 'Bob, you go with Jed. Leave me the lamp.'

'Suit yourself,' Oak said doubtfully. 'But I reckon you'd do better not to pull the old guy about. Just in case.'

'There's sense in that, Sal,' her brother said.

'Is that all Emilio Cruz's life amounted to?' the

girl asked indignantly.

'That's all any man's life adds up to when you come right down to it,' Oak said regretfully, putting the lamp into her hands and turning to where Jed had just struck a match and was lighting the candle.

'Come on, Bob,' Stokes said, shielding his newly sprung flame against the draught of his own movements. 'It's no good arguing with my sister.'

A door stood to the right of the fireplace. Jed Stokes opened it, and Oak followed him through into the kitchen. The room was clean enough, and had an iron cooking range and scrub-topped table. There was also a larder, but this contained little, though the store cupboard close to it was well stocked with vegetables and game that appeared to have been hung within the last week. But, apart from pots and pans and the usual household utensils, they came upon nothing else of interest, and had to unbar the back door and enter the shed outside before they located the set of gardening tools which contained the shovel they needed.

'Where do you plan to put him?' Jed asked, as they left the shed again.

'What's your idea?' Oak prompted.

'Figures he's got a nice soft vegetable garden,' Stokes answered. 'Most likely behind this shed.'

'I'm all for easy digging,' Oak acknowledged. 'Let's take a pasear.'

They walked to the back of the shed, where they found the plot of ground anticipated, and Oak promptly measured out a grave of average

dimensions and began to dig, the hole soon taking
shape and earth piling up beside it. But, not
content with a good start, he fairly threw himself
into the labour now, shovelling without pause for
the next half an hour, and he was more than three
feet into the earth when he called a halt and
sleeved off. After that he hopped out of the grave
and said to his companion: 'You can finish it.
Another foot or so ought to do it.'

Nodding, Stokes lowered himself into the grave
and took over the digging – which grew harder
with the top soil removed – and he spent the next
thirty minutes chopping out clay and stones and
sweating as much over his foot of progress as Oak
had over the previous three. When he stopped, it
was suddenly, and he tossed the shovel out of the
hole and declared: 'If hard exercise be more
acceptable than prayer, Emilio Cruz should walk
through heaven's gate on our recommendation.'

'It's deep enough,' Oak acknowledged, helping
Stokes out of the grave and standing by while the
man dusted himself off. 'Let's go back indoors and
get the body. The sooner we get this job finished,
the sooner we rest.'

Stokes yawned enormously. 'I'm almost too
tired to remember my name.'

'I forgot mine an hour ago,' Oak allowed
ironically, stepping round the shed to regain the
rear door of the dead Emilio's house.

Entering the dwelling, they passed through to
the living room, where Sally had the corpse laced
into a sheet and lying on top of the bed. The girl

herself was bending over the table, braced by her
arms, and clearly thinking deeply about an object
that lay before her.

'What's that, Sal?' her brother asked.

'I'm not sure,' the girl replied. 'It's gold, it's
beautiful, and Emilio was wearing it round his
neck. It's Aztec, I think.'

'Let's have a look,' Oak said, though Jed Stokes
had got to the object first and was now holding it
in his left hand and examining it closely in the
lamplight.

Stokes extended his palm, offering the golden
shape – which was about the same size as a
twenty-dollar gold piece – for joint inspection.
'What do you make of it, Bob?' he inquired. 'Did
you ever see its like before?'

'Yes, I believe I did,' Oak answered. 'It's Aztec
all right, and a sun charm. I knew a lady dealer up
in Denver who wore one like that – only nothing
like so heavy and perfect. She was the luckiest girl
with a pack of cards I ever did see. The face on the
disc – so she told me – is that of Quetzalcoatl, who
was sort of top gun among the Aztec gods.
Anybody who wears a sun charm is supposed to be
mighty fortunate in all aspects of life.'

'It seemed crazy to bury it up in the earth with
him,' Sally said. 'Did taking it from about his neck
amount to stealing from the dead?'

'He'd want you to have it,' Oak assured her. 'It's
thanks to you he'll be going into his grave decently
covered. Just so long as you don't sell the thing.
That can rile the dead, so I believe.'

'Take it and have done, Sally,' Jed Stokes advised. 'Emilio doesn't need it where he's gone, and you could surely do with a change of luck.'

'You could too, girl,' Oak said, turning to the shrouded figure on the bed. 'Get hold of his feet, Jed. Let's get him into the ground. There's the filling in to be done yet.'

'I'm coming with you,' Sally said.

'Please yourself,' Oak advised laconically, lifting the upper part of the corpse and looking round the top of his left arm as he steered for the kitchen door.

The burden put little strain on its two bearers. Emilio Cruz had not been a heavy man, and carrying him out to the ground at the back of the house took up no more than a minute. Holding the body in his arms, Oak slipped down into the grave and carefully laid the remains to rest. Then, after scrambling out again with Jed Stokes's help, he picked up the shovel and filled the hollow of its blade with dirt from the pile adjacent. 'Did you want to say something, Sally?' he asked.

'Just God rest his soul,' the girl responded, 'and may he find on the other side of life what he failed to find on this one.'

'Amen to that,' Oak said sincerely, tipping the contents of the shovel's blade into the hole.

'Amen,' Jed Stokes echoed firmly.

And a whine from the background – which told that the dog was present – concluded the vestigial burial service. After that the two men alternated with the task of shovelling earth into the grave, treading it down at intervals, and keeping up the work until the hole was filled in and the last of the displaced soil built into a low mound over the interment.

The two men took a short breather, then walked round to the front of Emilio Cruz's shed, Oak with the shovel in his grasp. 'Where's Sally?' he inquired, as he returned the tool to the spike from which it had originally been taken down.

'She went indoors several minutes ago,' Jed Stokes answered. 'She aimed to let as much air into the house as possible.'

Oak nodded. He saw no need to comment on that. They re-entered the dwelling – which was now full of draughts – and once more walked back through the kitchen and into the living room. Here Oak looked about him for Sally, wondering dully why she wasn't present; and then he saw the dog lying on his hearth and slowly perceived that it had rolled over in an abnormal manner. Going to the creature, he lifted its head, noticing blood at the corner of its mouth; and, while he believed the dog was still alive, he was fairly sure that it had been rendered unconscious by a blow on the head, probably struck with the barrel of a gun.

Looking up and round, Oak sought Jed Stokes's face, but realized that the other's reactions had been swifter than his own, for Stokes had already passed outside and started moving back and forth across the front of the house, calling his sister's name.

Jumping to it, Oak joined the other man

beneath the moon. 'The yelling won't do any good,' he advised tersely. 'Somebody has got her.'

And that somebody, as he knew very well, was Pete Brett.

Nine

But, despite Oak's tones, so blunt and command-
ing, Jed Stokes was in no mood to listen, and he
began to deepen his field of search, shouting
louder than ever. A presentiment of harm reared
within Oak as his companion approached the line
of darkness along the base of the slope that
reached back eastwards behind the flat ground
before the dwelling. Then a rifle banged, its flash
so vivid that it seemed to split Oak's sight, and
Stokes let out a thin scream, reached high, and
slipped to the earth, where he lay motionless
under a moonbeam.

Certain that tragedy had struck, Oak headed
for the collapsed figure, his steps accelerating into
a run; but his movements were abruptly checked
as the rifle spoke again and the bullet actually
stirred his hair in passing above him.

'That's more like it, Bob!' Pete Brett's once
familiar voice declared. 'I do hate being approached these days! You stay where you are, old
pal, and you'll take as little harm as this girl we've
got here!'

'Let her go, Pete,' Oak urged, 'and I'll come to you!'

'I'm pointing a gun at you,' Brett reminded. 'If I wanted it so, you'd come to me right now. But I don't want it so. All I want is for you to go back indoors and get yourself a good night's sleep. Tomorrow you can carry on as you'd planned.'

'Planned!' Oak exploded bitterly. 'What plans do you think I've got?'

'You'd better have some,' Buckley warned. 'And they'd better bear fruit. If they don't, Bob, this girl here – so safe and gently treated now – could come to a lot of harm in a very short time. Get me?'

'Oh, I get you all right!' Oak flung back. 'So we both know what I set out after, and I don't deny this is the place for it. Or was. 'Cos there's nothing here now. You ask Sally Stokes. She'll tell you. The Mission of San Miguel – the place the treasure was hidden – was buried under a landslide about sixty years ago.'

'So happens the girl has told us something of the sort,' Brett returned. 'You've got me wondering, but you haven't stopped me doubting. You're a clever one, Bob – or think you are – and you wouldn't have come here if you didn't still have some hope of finding what you set out to find.'

'Events forced us this way!' Oak snorted. 'We had to travel some place!'

'Don't that sound nice!' Brett jeered. 'You had to travel some place!'

'It's the simple truth, Pete!'

'It's simple!' Brett retorted. 'I remember you

and your innocent protests. Little wonder you
ended up behind bars! I'm telling you for the last
time! Don't try it on! You do your stuff tomorrow –
or it'll be death for you, and something worse for
the girl! I've got three strapping guys with me,
and they're all woman-hungry! You know what
that means!'

'I'll do my g'damned best!'

'You'll do better than that, Bob!'

'You treat that girl right.'

'As long as it pleases me.'

'Let me go to her brother, Pete.'

'He's dead,' Brett said. 'I shot to kill.'

'Cold-blooded murder!' Oak ground out. 'I swear
to heaven I'll kill you for that!'

'You may not live that long,' Brett cautioned.
'Remember whose finger is on the trigger right
now.'

'No sweat, Pete!' Oak taunted. 'You'll have to
put up with it. I've got something you need.'

'Don't you go presuming a whole heap on that,'
Brett advised, his tones now flattened by a chill
note of warning. 'There's no telling what the girl
knows, and what I might be able to torture out of
her.' He paused to let his words sink in. 'Now I'm
sick of listening to the sound of your voice. Go
back indoors, and do what I told you – and not
another word!'

Oak faced about. He saw no point in provoking
further. The man could be as unpredictable as he
was cruel when he reached the limit of his
tolerance. Sally might have to suffer if he wound

the guy up that fraction more. His time would
come. He'd yet avenge Jed's murder, and the
insults to the girl. The iron had entered his soul.
For the first time in his life Oak was certain that
he could face Pete Brett and win. So why risk
throwing it all away on one more futile jibe?

Walking back into the house, Oak left the front
door open behind him. There was an armchair on
the right of the hearth, and he sank into it, closing
his eyes and stretching out his legs. Besides being
exhausted, he felt stunned. Jed's death had come
so suddenly, and at the height of the poor devil's
anxiety for his sister. It was as if something of the
greatest good had earned the greatest evil. How
could a man believe in the existence of a just and
loving God when such things happened? How,
indeed, could a man believe in anything that had
a higher purpose than human selfishness?

A movement near Oak's feet caused him to open
his eyes again. The dog that he had seen lying
there earlier – and of which he had taken no
account on coming back indoors – had just
recovered its senses and stood up. Black as
midnight, except for the white blaze in the middle
of its forehead, it poised unsteadily on palsied
joints, gave itself a feeble shake, and wobbled over
to the now vacant bed. Then it dragged itself
weakly up from the floor and collapsed on the foot
of the coverlet, either unconscious again or dead;
but Oak felt too far gone himself to care which,
and simply shut his eyes once more and let go. Yet
sleep would not come.

It troubled him that he, Jed, and Sally had made such a mess of the daylight hours. They had been tricked, and none too subtly at that. Most of the time Pete Brett had been much closer to them than he, Oak, had believed the facts of travel allowed. How? Why, simply when you came to think about it. They had kept watch from start to finish on the belief that any threat to them must either be travelling the high rock on their left or the land directly in their wake. This meant that they had covered only two facets of their back-trail, and never bothered to look behind them and out to the west.

How easy it must have been for the shadowing Brett to have descended from the heights, ridden out onto the flats – which were not really all that flat – and then swung southwards and kept the fugitives under observation through his spy-glass. The probability was that, when Jed Stokes had initiated what he had regarded as his crafty swing away from the mountains in the dusk, Pete Brett and company had been close enough to see at least something of what had happened and to manoeuvre as necessary. Then, riding parallel through the night on a more northerly line, they had most likely been attracted by the barking of the dog in the same manner as it had drawn in the trio already en route for San Miguel. It all seemed so obvious now that Oak could not credit how he had failed to get a glimmering of how badly he and his companions had been fouling up as they rode here. No wonder Brett had treated him with such

contempt. The man must be feeling very pleased
with himself at this time.

But it was all water down the creek now, and it
was what happened from this point on that
mattered. He must watch for his opening against
Brett; if he kept vigilant it would surely come.
With that, his mind stopped churning and he fell
asleep.

He awoke to a room that was filled with the
morning light. Looking about him a trifle dazedly,
he wondered at his surroundings, and then his
memory returned and plunged him back into the
morass of problems and fears from which he had
escaped not so long ago. If only a man could sleep
the dangerous years away; but he was no Rip Van
Winkle. He must rise and face the day, knowing
that his life was in the balance. If he could not
produce some kind of miracle in the hours ahead,
it would be a permanent lights out for him and
Sally Stokes.

Forcing himself erect, Oak rubbed his eyes and
almost dislocated his jaw with a cavernous yawn.
Then he shambled over to the door and, propping
himself off its frame by the length of his arms,
peered out. He saw the horses which he and the
Stokes pair had ridden to this place. The brutes,
never tied, had strayed apart and were cropping
as and where grass was to be found. He saw Jed
Stoke's body too. It lay just as he remembered
from the moonlight, except that now its lines had
stiffened. But of Pete Brett and company there
was nothing to be seen, and he could have been

alone with the curving bluffs and the slope that went stretching away eastwards beyond the ruins of the village and the lower ground itself, but he knew that he wasn't. Brett was out there all right, and most likely had him in sight at this very moment.

Of the mind to put it to the test, Oak was tempted to walk over to his horse and see whether he drew fire, but just then he heard a whining at his back and looked round and down. The black dog was standing there, eyes filled with a friendly light and tail wagging. So the creature hadn't died. Well, he was glad of it. The dog made a friend and ally in this hour of doubt and loneliness. 'Hi, feller!' he greeted. 'Glad to see you made it. Another tough old coot, eh?'

The dog licked his outstretched hand, then dashed past him, trotted a few circles outside, and cocked its leg before going further afield to take care of more intimate matters. Smiling wryly to himself at the normalcy of it all, Oak turned away from the door and sauntered through to the kitchen, still racked by yawns but slowly finding energy and complete wakefulness.

He found a bucket of water in a corner of the pantry. It was clean stuff and fit to drink. Then, with his thirst slaked, he located a stone jug and dipped out a quart of the cold liquid, pouring it straight over his head and shaking himself as the chill registered down the length of him and he shivered. Now he nosed out a very dry loaf of rye bread and a few wizened apples. It was poor sustenance, but he consumed it gratefully and then sleeved off his mouth, reckoning that he was once more capable of serious thought.

Yet what had he to think about? – that was the question. He had been told what was expected of him, and had the wit to know that he must do it. For the rest, he still had his gun; though, with Sally Stokes in Brett's hands, he could imagine few circumstances in which he would be likely to risk using it. But was he giving up too much on the girl's account? He could be submitting to a sense of misguided responsibility and warped chivalry. Pete Brett was assuming that he, Oak, owed Sally something, but in fact he didn't. The girl was just a pretty face, and the pathetic case of the moment. Indeed, when you came right down to it, she was no saint and, whatever the excuses for her, there were better women rotting in jail.

Here was another temptation. He was reasonably certain that he could grab a horse and make a bolt for it into the open country north of San Miguel. He had every right to save his own life – since he reckoned that both Sally *and* he would have to die if he stayed on – and he could think of no hard and practical man of his acquaintance who would blame him for leaving a woman of her kind to meet her own fate. After all, rape had always been part of the female experience and its cruel indignities would in this case by erased by a final bullet. It was a bad world. Men were no better than animals. Self alone counted. He had remarked it before – and so had everybody else. It was the only sane code to live by.

Then he saw the dog again. The animal was sitting at the middle of the kitchen floor and gazing up at him expectantly. 'Oh, that's it, is it?' he said. 'I'm the boss now. Damned if you aren't a better man than the rest of us put together! Never ran out once in your life where you were needed, did you? Come on, then. Let's go and have a look round. I don't see what the hell good it's going to do, but – let's go and do it anyway.'

They left the house by the back door. Needing an unrestricted view, Oak moved clear of the shed at the dwelling's rear and took in the huge crescent of land which met the base of the cliffs that swung across the western background. His gaze soon fixed on the summit rock which dominated the cliff formation from somewhere to the left of centre, deciding that it had been here – to judge from the torn convexity of the rockfaces under the pinnacle – that the great landslide had occurred which had swept away the Spanish Mission that had undoubtedly been the pivot of life in this now derelict place at the start of the century.

With the dog romping on ahead, sniffing and darting – and showing little of the previous night's harm to its skull – Oak walked towards the ground beneath the summit, his recent judgment confirmed by the vast mound of earth and stone which he saw canted there into a final pattern of spillage that left visible the ends of the table-rock on which the mission building itself

must originally have been erected. Altogether, as
he studied the damage, he had the feeling – first
experienced while watching a destructive boy at
play among the sandcastles – that here a work
built with love and care had been abruptly swept
flat by a hand as uncaring as it was violent. But the
story of San Miguel was not a new one, and it would
be repeated here and there for as long as storm and
earthquake exercised their power on human
affairs.

Coming to the pile, Oak went at once to its rear
northern corner, then reversed course and walked
slowly around the whole of its ragged base, ending
in the rear southern corner. After that he scrambled to the top of the heap, wandered about up
there for a minute or two – again seeing nothing
that he had not expected to see – and then climbed
down its front, his canine friend often in close
attendance but sometimes not; and he was getting
ready to throw up his hands in a gesture of resig-
nation and hopelessness for the expected watch-
ers, when he realized that the dog had vanished
altogether.

Aware, but in no sense worried, he pursed his
lips in a brief whistle – the very first time that he
had used this summons – and he was startled
when the dog, with audible scrambling, suddenly
reappeared out of a hole nearby, at the foot of the
mound, and looked up at him in its usual inquiring
manner. 'What the deuce are you after in there?'
Oak asked. 'No rabbit would live in that earth, and
a fox would have more sense. Would it be rats,

then? Ah, I reckon that's it!'

The dog gazed at him with real intelligence. He received a powerful impression that it understood why he was here and wanted to show him something important. Bending, he peered into the hole from which it had just emerged, perceiving now that the orifice had been deliberately reduced in size by the cunning use of wadded sackcloth, hay, and rocks masked with dirt. The work was carefully done, and reasoned. No brutish intelligence had been responsible for this. A human hand had been employed here. Emilio Cruz's almost certainly.

Kneeling, Oak pulled the packing out of the hole. Then he thrust his head into the aperture, seeing that a fissure went plunging back and down through the bottom of the materials which the landslide had deposited here so long ago. He entered the rift, not finding it so different from a symmetrical tunnel, and crawled inwards for perhaps ten feet, conscious that the dark was rising densely now and would soon enclose him.

He checked his movements. It would be madness to go any further without a light. He must go and get one straightaway. He seemed to remember having seen a lantern in Emilio Cruz's shed the night before. Back then; and he reversed motion – emerging hot and dusty in the morning cool shortly afterwards, and feeling an excitement which took little account of the telescope that was most probably directed at him from some vantage on the slope yonder.

The walk back to the house took about ten minutes. He found the lantern in the shed, as he had expected. Realizing the possible danger of what he was about to undertake, he saw it necessary to check the lantern for oil and an adequate wick; so there could be no doubt that more than half an hour had elapsed when he and the dog halted once again before the orifice and he rummaged out a match and crouched down to fire the wick of his stormlight.

Intent on what he was doing, Oak picked up no sound from his back, and he was preparing to thrust the lantern deep into the rift before him, when the muzzle of a pistol jarred against the base of his skull and a swift hand relieved him of the Colt on his right hip. 'Take it easy, Bob!' a voice that he knew for Pete Brett's cautioned. 'What have you found?'

'Fool question to ask!' Oak snorted. 'You know as much about it as I do.'

'Well, just maybe,' Brett allowed. 'You'd better stand up. I'd hate to see you get an old man's knee before your time. If you've got much left anyhow.'

'Bless your heart, Peter,' Oak said, straightening. 'Where's the girl?'

'I've left her with Ray and Joey Milligan,' Brett answered. 'She'll be safe with them.'

'A female gorilla wouldn't be safe with them!'

'You disappoint me, Bob,' Brett sighed. 'You've lost all faith in your fellow man.'

'That's because I've never heard the Milligan twins so described,' Oak retored sourly. 'I suppose you aim to come in there with me?'

'You suppose dead right,' Brett replied. 'What's more, there won't be a gun between us.'

'I'm sure there'll be one waiting out here.'

'In the capable hand of Lem Defors,' Pete Brett agreed, moving the muzzle of his gun from the back of Oak's head. 'Turn round and say morning to Lem.'

Oak craned, scowling at the whiskery, hardbitten six-footer who stood at Brett's left shoulder. 'Good morning, Lem.'

'You want your butt kicked, Oak?' Defors rasped.

'He's a brave man with a forty-four in his mitt!' Oak jeered.

'Pick up that lantern,' Brett ordered, 'and shut your mouth! I still can't abide the sound of your voice!'

'What a shame,' Oak sighed, plucking the lantern off the ground and this time thrusting it deep into the rift before them. 'Do you want to lead or follow?'

'I'll follow,' Brett said shortly. 'That way I'll be able to keep an eye on you.'

'Don't forget to leave your hogleg with Defors.'

'You juicing me?' Brett demanded, handing over his revolver to the man beside him.

'Dead serious,' Oak retorted. 'Heaven knows what the vibrations of a gunshot might do where we're going. If we're really going anywhere that is. But that's what we've got to see, isn't it?'

'In you go!' Brett commanded.

Oak crawled into the cleft. Gathering the

lantern, he went nosing forward and down, soon passing what he believed to have been the point that he had reached during his earlier brief descent into the rift. Inching ahead on his elbows and knees, he felt the joints beginning to smart and realized that they wouldn't take much skinning in these tight and abrasive conditions; but he was not required to crawl much further in this way, for the debris of the landslide suddenly gave place to what was plainly a stone wall that had split wide open before the same impacting forces which had created the rest of the passage-like crack. 'You okay back there?' he asked of Brett, spitting dirt and finding it difficult to breathe in the stifling conditions. 'It appears to me we're reached what's left of the mission. Looks like there's a drop ahead. We may need a rope.'

'We haven't got one,' Brett snarled. 'Push on.'

Oak eased his arms and torso through the riven wall, and the light from the lantern revealed space all around and a floor about three feet below his nose. Had his body been reversed, the drop would have been negotiated as a matter of course and meant nothing to speak of; but going into it headfirst made the difference. Setting the lantern down well clear of his estimated point of arrival, Oak let himself fall through the broken wall and, landing on his right shoulder, rolled clumsily. But, although shaken up, he was unhurt and able to twist round and help Brett down after him with such nonchalance that the other man seemed unaware that an obstacle had been overcome.

Looking up and around him in evident amazement, Brett came erect in the small circle of light cast by the lantern on the floor. 'The place is still standing,' he said. 'It got buried as it stood.'

'Doubt not,' Oak said, picking up and raising the lantern again, its more widely spread light now revealing drunken angles, a much cracked floor, heaps of powdered adobe, compressed walls, and a ceiling that slanted down from a height of twelve feet above their heads to a frill of indescribable ruin running at floor level about twenty feet beyond. 'It was a real freak outcome, I guess. Who'd have imagined it from the mound outside?'

'Is it safe?'

Oak blinked at the other. 'You have to ask a dumb thing like that? Hell, no!'

'Then what are we standing about for?' Brett demanded. 'We're treasure hunting, aren't we? Where exactly do we look, Bob?'

It was the 'exactly' that had Oak baffled. His first concern had been to confirm the existence of the mission, and his second to find it. He had been quite happy to let those larger considerations fill his mind. No man reduced his problems to the final detail before he had to, and it was likely that he had believed in his heart that he would never be required to concentrate on the minutiae of the matter. Yet now, totally against the run of possibility, they were actually standing inside what was left of a building that had disappeared from the world outside two generations ago.

'The treasure might be anywhere or nowhere,' he answered. 'Fact is, Pete, I've no notion where to look.'

Ten

Oak waited for it, aware that his companion was choking and spluttering on an anger that he could not yet express.

'Well, that's a nice thing to tell a man!' Brett finally exploded. 'Great day, Bob! You simply don't enter into a thing as important as this without giving it some real thought first!'

'I had you to think about, mister!' Oak reminded sourly. 'Then came the Stokes pair and the people they'd riled back in the mountains. I had my share to think about!'

'You and your damned excuses!' Brett roared disdainfully. 'Did I hear you pronouncing on Ray and Joey Milligan just now? They've got brains in their heads compared with you!'

'You're behaving like a spoiled kid!' Oak retaliated. 'You need your backside paddled! Can't you stomach a bit of disappointment? Grow up, damn your eyes, and think about it!' He added a few quick sentences to explain how rough and readily Richard Giles's map had been produced, ending: 'Even if Colonel Bayward had come here

in those early days, he'd still have had to seek on
the principle of "by guess and by God".'

'Where's that goldurned map?' Brett demanded,
not the least mollified. 'I suppose you haven't got
it, eh? A great, blundering, mixed-up critter like
you would lose his own shadow of a sunny
evening!'

'We're here,' Oak reflected, thrusting a hand
into the pocket where he kept the map. 'Just you
and me – a pair of damned fools, like as not! Here
you are – here's the map. Have a look at it, and
maybe you'll see what I mean.'

Brett snatched the piece of vellum out of Oak's
grasp. Then, bending towards the lantern, he
opened the map and began studying it intently.
'So it's not a map Frémont would have been proud
of,' he finally allowed. 'But it's plain enough. It's
your thick skull that's lacking. I keep telling you!'

'Then you'd better tell me,' Oak advised
patiently.

'The arrow, man!' Brett snapped. 'Don't you see?'

'Sure, it points to San Miguel,' Oak said. 'To the
mission. Even if it does lack true reckoning.'

'It points to the cross.'

'Sure. Isn't that how they mark a church on a
map, Pete?'

'Where do you see a cross?'

'On a roof – at the trailside, maybe – over a
grave.'

'Usually, man – usually?' Brett protested.

Oak shrugged.

'Standing on an altar.'

Oak couldn't quarrel with that, and he had to admit to himself that he had been slow in the matter. 'I wonder if the altar is still standing?'

'There's only one way to find out,' Brett reminded, pointing to his left. 'It'd be that way.'

With dust sifting through the air about them, they began a slow advance under the dull glow of the storm-lantern, the shadows behind the nightmarish distortions of the ancient hall suggesting an ante-room in hell – and then they came face to face with Death himself, the hair rising on Oak's nape and Brett letting out a yell of fright. For the Bony One was a fearsome sight indeed. He leered at them from within the cowl of a black habit, and his skeletal arms reached out of wide sleeves to embrace them.

'G'dammit!' Pete Brett flared, leaping in and swinging a fist – and the skull went flying and the habit came fluttering down amidst a rattling of bones.

'I do believe you were scared,' Oak observed cynically, grinning at his companion's ashen features. 'Somebody's little joke. Didn't you twig it?'

'Somebody's little –' the other began, recovering himself with a visible effort. 'You mean –?'

'Only what should have been fairly evident from the start,' Oak replied soberly. 'Somebody was here before us. I reckon you saw me pull out the stuff packed into the mouth of the tunnel back there. That sacking and the rest of it didn't get stuck in the opening by chance. I'd never have

spotted anything if the dog hadn't shown me.
Good job you failed to kill the poor brute last
night.'

'It went for me,' Brett retorted.

'I reckon you started it.'

'Damned mongrel!' Brett snorted dismissively.

'It had a master,' Oak said significantly.

'Where is he?'

'Dead. We found him so. Jed Stokes and I buried
him last night.'

'You figure that skeleton set-up was his work?'

'Everything points to it,' Oak said. 'I guess he
strung up the remains of one of the holy fathers to
frighten off anybody else who happened to find
their way in here.'

'Protecting the treasure?'

'Again,' Oak said uncertainly, 'that's how it
looks.'

Brett snatched the lantern out of Oak's grasp
and resumed moving forward. He trampled on the
bones of the dead. Skirting the remains, Oak
followed him into the darkness ahead, and they
came to three steps which led up to the altar and
the undamaged ebony cross which surmounted it.
Pausing at the foot of the steps, Oak let his
companion ascend and have the space about the
altar to himself. Then Brett set the lantern on the
left-hand side of the bench and began to examine
the crucifix – lifting it, shaking it, and attempting
to force it this way or that – and suddenly he
discovered that the cross itself was a fixture, but
that the altar could be lifted back from the wall

against which it stood as a whole, and that when this was done an area of raw earth appeared low down and showed signs of having been excavated more than once. 'I think this is what we were looking for,' Brett observed, a note of triumph in his voice.

Oak nodded. He watched the other crouch and start digging at the soil with his hands. A grunt escaping him almost at once, Brett worked harder and harder, his movements becoming quite feverish as he first uncovered and then dragged out a small but heavy-looking walnut chest that was bound with brass bands.

Lifting the chest now, Brett placed it on the altar and examined its lid. This was secured with interlocking loops of metal and a pin. Removing the pin, he raised the lid and peered into the chest, murmuring a vague disappointment as he retreated to the lowest of the steps and gestured for Oak to ascend and occupy the place which he had just vacated.

Oak climbed up to the altar. He shoved it back against the wall, then looked into the chest. He saw what was undoubtedly a silver altar service. There was jewelled chalice for the wine and a beautifully chased plate for the Host. A valuable-looking ring, possibly a bishop's, was also present, as were one or two other pieces that ought to sell for a good price, but Oak was pretty sure that the silverwork was Spanish in origin and had as little to do with the Aztec people as did the shirt on his back. 'This is all there was?' he asked, craning at Brett.

Brett gave his chin a jerk. 'I was careful.'

'Not what we expected,' Oak said; 'but not bad for a morning's work all the same. Ten thousand dollars?'

'Maybe,' Brett answered, his blue eyes smiling coldly out of his slightly wolfish face. 'You're not expecting a cut?'

'You murdered my uncle,' Oak said. 'You murdered Jed Stokes last night. But you've got what you wanted now. Where's the sense murdering anybody else? Better men than you have ended up swinging.'

'I seem to remember you said you were going to kill me,' Brett remarked. 'You're not man enough by half, but I have to protect myself.'

'Face me then,' Oak urged. 'Draw-and-shoot.'

'Wouldn't you like?' Brett scoffed. 'You know me, Bob. I never take unnecessary chances, and who's to say what happened to you west of the Black mountains?'

'Let the girl go,' Oak said sternly. 'You owe me that much. You'd never have found this place if I hadn't led you here.'

'Another of your weak arguments,' Brett commented. 'I owe you no favours, mister. Not after the trouble you put me to in Coopville and since. Just stop your persuading. I'm not going to listen to anything you say.' Then he laughed savagely. 'But I will offer you a word of advice. If you stand up and take it like a man, it's over before you know it. You won't feel a thing.'

'It isn't over yet, Pete.'

'Why do men say silly things like that,' Brett inquired, 'when they know good and well it is? You bore me, Bob. You always did.' He spat to emphasize his feelings. 'Let's get out of this stinking tomb. You go first again.'

'What about the chest?'

'Yeah, it's heavy,' Brett agreed. 'It'd take the two of us to handle it. I'm not going to give you the smallest chance to brew up trouble. No, sir! I'll send the Milligan twins in here for that.'

Oak picked up the lantern again. As ever, Pete Brett had been his match. Biting his lip, he carried the light back down the length of the semi-collapsed hall, its oily glow flitting on and off the dusty stone surfaces lurching amidst the banks of stygian gloom, and he regained the inner mouth of the tunnel which led back to the just discernible daylight not too far above.

Once more placing the light ahead of him, Oak dipped back into the cleft and, with a writhe and twist of his torso, started his return to the open air. It proved a far more difficult and laborious climb than he had expected – though he might have known that, in the nature of things, getting out would be harder than getting in – and he picked up his share of scrapes and scratches, but he finally thrust his head out of the rift and hung there, panting.

The dog was standing nearby. It moved in and licked his face. But Lem Defors – who was placed even closer to the hole – promptly kneed the creature aside and seized Oak by the collar,

146   *He Died With His Boots Off*

hauling him bodily out of the passage and
dumping him on his face. 'Keep down!' he ordered.

'What the heck's the matter?' Oak spluttered.

Defors' only reply was to place the sole of a boot
on the back of the prisoner's skull and force Oak's
forehead to the ground, holding it there; and it
was not until Brett emerged from the passage a
few moments later that he learned what was
going on; for Defors blurted out: 'We got trouble
yonder, Pete! I believe them Milligan boys have
done got killed!'

'Hey?' Brett gasped, rising to his knees and
using both palms to wipe the sweat and dirt from
his eyes. 'How was that again?'

'Some fellers rid up from the east a short while
ago,' Defors explained. 'It looked to me like they
started a quarrel with Ray and Joey over the
Stokes girl. Anyhow they all got to shooting. The
Milligans got two or three of them horsemen, but
the horsemen also got Ray and Joey. I saw 'em go
down, and they haven't got up again.'

Brett gave vent to some filthy swearing. 'Must
be that bunch we saw hunting Oak and the other
two yesterday,' he observed, when he calmed
down. 'A patched and flea-bit lot. I didn't give
them credit for that much savvy or stick. Seems I
made a mistake there.'

'The Milligans sure did,' Defors said heavily.

'How many of them are there?'

'Now? Five or six.'

'Figures some of that party must have slid off
home.'

'So what?'

'Do they know we're over here?' Brett snapped.

'Can't say for sure,' Defors responded. 'I figure they must. I saw Ray Milligan point this way. But –'

'But what?'

'They're all hunkered about that guy Stokes's body right now.'

'Carrion,' Brett sniffed. 'Let Oak up.'

Defors removed his foot from the back of Oak's head.

'What was it with the Stokeses?' Brett asked.

'They were a pair of local crooks,' Oak replied. 'There's a town not so far from here. Presterville. The folk from there set out to nail Jed and Sally Stokes. You probably know I saved the two of them from being strung up.'

'It seems you did them no favours,' Brett growled thoughtfully. 'Nor yourself for the matter of that.' He glanced at Defors. 'What say to this, Lem? D'you figure those bastards will go away if we give them Oak?'

'Maybe,' Defors said, his weathered brow corrugated. 'But I wouldn't bet money on it, Pete. They have to be mighty curious about us already.'

'What us – a posse from up river?'

'Out of our jurisdiction?' Defors queried. 'Do possemen shoot folk who ride up on them?'

'Why not?' Brett inquired brazenly. 'The world's full of mistakes. I can carry off a bluff if you can. We can apologise for the Milligans.'

'Him?' Defors asked, nodding at Oak. 'He isn't

goin' to keep his mouth shut.'

'Who's going to listen to him?' Brett said archly.
'He saved the Stokeses, didn't he?'

'You're the boss, Pete,' Defors said with finality,
'and I'm right behind you.'

'Back me up,' Brett acknowledged. 'Back me up,
Lem, and we'll be okay!'

Defors gestured with his gun barrel for the cap-
tive to rise. Oak jacked himself upright, as Brett
did the same, and the three of them – with the dog
skirting wide – began heading towards the base of
the nearby eastern slope and the men from Presterville. The latter had just packed Jed Stokes's
grotesquely stiffened corpse onto a horse and were
now looking towards the area from which Brett
and company had begun advancing. Oak saw the
square-bodied, well-dressed figure of Nicolas
Dumont standing out in front of his four companions and clearly asking himself – as he held a
cocked revolver at the ready on his unwounded left
wing – what the oncoming men had in mind.

'Good morning, sir,' Brett called politely.

'Good morning,' came Dumont's response in well
modulated tones. 'Kindly halt, and stay where you
are.'

'Why, certainly,' Brett answered, stopping his
trio about a dozen yards short of Dumont's party. 'I
owe you an apology, sir. Those two boys of mine
must have supposed you were trying to rescue
their prisoner.'

'That won't do,' the other retorted. 'There are
dead men to answer for. Who are you?'

'Sheriff Chet Allan,' Brett replied readily. 'Of Los Luanas – up the river. My deputy, Lem Defors.'

'Los Luanas, eh?' Dumont said suspiciously. 'I visit there now and again. Los Luanas has no Sheriff Chet Allan.'

'Not of the election two weeks back?' Brett queried. 'When did you last visit Los Luanas, sir?'

'Three months ago.'

'A lot has happened up there since then.'

'No doubt,' Dumont conceded. 'From whom did you take over, Mr Allan?'

'I'm beginning not to like this,' Brett warned, stiffly aggrieved. 'I'd hate to think you didn't trust me, sir.'

'Where's your badge?'

'I had some crawling to do over at the mound,' Brett explained, glancing down at his chest. 'I must have lost it. I hadn't noticed until you asked. I see the reason for your doubt. I'd wonder in your place.'

'What were you crawling about for?' Dumont demanded.

'I was searching for the grave of a man this prisoner of ours – Bob Oak – murdered.'

'When?'

'A while back.'

'How did you come to know about it?'

'We – we're the law,' Brett spluttered. 'We were informed. Now I've been patient –'

'By whom?'

'The man you found lying dead over there – Jed

Stokes,' Brett answered glibly. 'The fact he told me was the reason why Oak shot him last night.'

'Now I know you're a liar,' Dumont said grimly. 'My party and I were close by you last night. We were content to watch and wait. We have a fair idea of what happened. Stokes was shot from your side.'

'Prove it!' Brett snapped. 'You haven't dealt honestly with me, whoever you are!'

'You,' Dumont said, looking frostily at Oak. 'What have you got to say? What's over there? Is it a grave?'

Defors jabbed the muzzle of his revolver deep into Oak's side. 'Not a word!' he cautioned. 'You're an arrested man!'

'That's right, Lem,' Brett agreed self-righteously. 'A man under arrest can only give evidence to an officer of the court.'

'Take that gun off him!' Dumont warned, half turning his head. 'You men cover Mr Chet Allan. I'll have the truth of this before I've done.'

'One more word,' Defors threatened, 'and I'll shoot the prisoner.'

'You'll die in the process,' Dumont said just as harshly, adjusting his aim. 'You can't shoot in two directions at once, deputy – also without a badge.'

Oak tensed. It was going to be a nice little stand-off; but his instinct told him that, if he didn't act now – while all his enemies were more concerned with each other than with him – he was going to die, at this turn of the situation or that, both tamely and suddenly. He knew where his

gun was. It had been thrust into the top of Defors'
trousers – placed about as nicely as it could be –
and Oak spun to his left, coming instantly off the
muzzle of his guard's weapon. Passing across the
front of Defors' body, he whipped his Colt out of the
other's waistband. After that he whirled to a halt
about two yards beyond his surprised captors and
blasted at Pete Brett, who had made a desperate
turn towards him and was preparing to gun him
down. His bullet flew higher than he had intended,
while Brett's travelled wide, but blood and flesh
flew off his enemy's head and Brett toppled backwards as rigidly as a severed tree and appeared
dead forever.

There were more detonations. Oak saw that
Dumont and Defors had fired at each other simultaneously. Dumont crumpled, a scarlet rose blos-
soming over his heart at an impossible rate, and
Defors staggered before a grazing hit across the
right side of his ribs; but the man went on shooting,
mouth and eyes wide open, as the men from Presterville pumped lead revengefully in his direction.

Somebody triggered at Oak. He shrank from the
hissing lead, wanting no further part in this fight –
since he found it hard to regard the men over the
way as enemies – but he had indeed been part of
their hunt and was no less surely included in this
showdown. So he fired back with a will, knowing
that a man who wished to survive must put his all
into battling with a gun, and he immediately broke
the right shoulder of a townsman with a deliberately placed shot.

Then he saw that Defors had sunk to his knees. The man was bleeding from a number of injuries, but still snarling his defiance and shooting his pistol. He had dropped one townsman and wounded another. Oak realized that it was almost over with Defors, and he sought another target opposite the man, but another revolver cut loose at that moment and slugs went flying amidst the remaining townsmen. The leaden hail scared the wits out of them, but it did no further harm, and those still capable of it broke and ran for their horses. Now Defors keeled over and died, Oak lowered his Colt, and the latest gun discharged its final bullet.

Oak looked round to find out who had been responsible for the outburst of wild shooting which had concluded the fight, and he saw Sally Stokes standing at the foot of the nearby slope – close to the horse that bore her brother's corpse indeed – and he formed the impression that she had seized the gun which had been left in the dead man's holster, pointed it in the right direction, and triggered off all six shots in the best manner she could.

Watching the townsmen, wounded and whole alike, driving their horses up the grade in all-out flight, Oak strolled over to Sally, who simply dropped her gun at the sight of him and hung her head. 'Oh, Bob,' she murmured.

'Chin up, girl!' he exhorted. 'That leaves you, me and dog, and I'm damned if we aren't the right three together!'

'Poor Jed.'

'Can't change anything, Sally,' he reminded, his sympathy of the gravest sort as he gripped her gently by the left arm. 'Let's go over to old Cruz's house.'

'What for?'

'Maybe nothing,' he said, pausing to whistle the dog. 'Perhaps all the luck there ever was in an Aztec sun charm.'

Eleven

It had taken Oak a couple of hours to find it.
Emilio Cruz had been clever enough to create a
hiding place at once obvious and yet unlikely to
draw anybody's attention.

There was a cupboard built into the wall behind
the bed and to the left of the fireplace. It had a
wooden floor and walls, and contained neatly
folded linen and old garments. Oak had emptied
the cupboard at the start of his search, and run an
eye over its apparently solid interior – tapping at
the walls and floor with his knuckles – but he had
seen no suspicious joins and had raised no hollow
echoes, so he had quickly decided that he was
wasting his time in this particular quarter and
passed on.

He had told Sally by then what he was looking
for. Thereafter, deliberately duplicating each
other's efforts, they had gone through the entire
house and shed outside, seeking across the floors,
around the walls, in the fireplace, up the chimney,
and beneath the doorsteps. There were many
other places too, but their work drew constant

disappointment, and it was only when Oak returned to that first cupboard and made a second inspection of its floor that he glimpsed what he had missed before.

The floor appeared to have been constructed in one piece, but this was not really so. In fact it had been put together in sound-dulling layers of clapboard and fibre. Careful work with a rubstone and paint pot had afterwards added the impression of solidity to the part of the job facing into the room; but, once a knife-blade had revealed what a sham it all was, there had been little to prising out these upper layers and uncovering the foundation of blocked timbers beneath.

Watched by Sally and the dog, Oak had removed these blocks and dug a few inches into the sandy dirt beneath, quickly locating a fairly large object wrapped in oilskin. It had taken a little while to fully unearth his find and lift it out onto the living room floor; but removing the oilskin had been no problem, and the object bared had proved to be a graven native box of some antiquity.

Certain that his patience and astuteness had been rewarded, Oak had lifted the lid of the box to reveal diadems studded with blue diamonds, necklaces of sapphires and emeralds, gold and silver bracelets and bangles, rings, torques, buckles and much else, all valuable singly and worth a great fortune as a whole. 'Maybe a million dollars!' Oak had breathed at the first sight; and he was still marvelling at the incredible figure

which had branded itself upon his brain. 'I knew it
had to be here, Sally,' he now went on. 'That Aztec
sun charm was the clue. It had to be a piece from a
genuine treasure. Cruz had most likely been
poking around under that mound for years. He
probably found this boxful ages ago. The stuff he
hid in its place was neither more nor less than the
mission silver. I guess we shall never know why
he did that. He had no cause that I can see to
anticipate a searcher. I doubt he saw a visitor
from one ten-year to the next.'

'Maybe he had second sight,' the girl suggested.
'Or perhaps there was some kind of message left
with the treasure.'

'The second sight stuff I can't buy,' Oak said
dismissively; 'but the other is a possibility.
Enough, anyway, to suggest why Cruz might have
seen the need to protect his find with a little
Mexican craft.' He twitched a shoulder. 'Oh, what
the hell! We've got it, Sally. And when I've
delivered Heidi's cut to her, you and I can start
thinking what we're going to do with ours.'

The dog growled. Oak saw that the creature
was looking towards the door, and that its hackles
were up. Straightening out of the crouch that he
had occupied for too long, Oak started reaching
for his pistol, but at that instant a big figure –
bloody, lank-haired, and wild-eyed, – came
bursting across the threshold, and floundered to a
halt, left hand propping him off the table at the
centre of the room while he covered Oak with the
Colt in his right. 'You aren't going to do anything

with it!' he mouthed, the girl screaming nearby as she pointed at the brain pulsing in his blasted and misshapen head. 'You're going to lie here and rot into a heap of white bones! I'm going to take that treasure home with me and spend it on a lifetime of fun! Did you imagine I was deceived about it down there in the mission, Bob?'

'You're dead, Pete!' Oak retorted aghast. 'Whatever you may think, you're dead!'

'Am I, by God!' Brett raved, pointing his revolver unsteadily at Oak's torso. 'I'll show you!'

Snarling, the dog launched itself off the floor. It struck Brett between the chest and throat, knocking him backwards, and he fell against the wall behind him and then crashed to the floor, his Colt detonating at the ceiling and causing plaster to shower down.

Oak whipped out his pistol. He was determined to make no mistake this time. Aiming for a split second, he sent a bullet through Brett's heart, and then he sent another after it; and when the gunsmoke cleared, the badman had lurched over into the angle formed by the floor and wall and lay lifeless.

Thrusting his pistol away, Oak walked over to the dog and fondled its head. 'Thanks, boy,' he said. 'You got your own back, and we saw him off. That was Pete Brett, the terror of New Mexico – or so he thought.'

'I can't stay in here a moment longer,' the girl said faintly, stumbling to the door and then outside.

Oak couldn't blame her. What Sally had seen this morning was more than enough to sicken the average woman. It might even be that she was coming to regard him as just another killer. Here again he would find it hard to blame her, but she must realize that he had only done what had to be done. He had fired shots only to keep them alive. Well, she must come to terms with it all according to her lights. Picking up the box of Aztec treasure, he moved in the direction that Sally Stokes had already gone, and the dog trotted after him.

It was the noon of the following day. They had passed through the southern end of the mountains and cut the Deming trail. Oak had already divided the treasure up, and made two bundles of it. One bundle he aimed to take up the Rio Grande and deliver to Heidi in Coopville, while the other Sally Stokes had just packed into a saddlebag.

'I know we've talked this out before,' Oak said, 'but if there's anything about our arrangements that you don't like, you'd better say so before we part.'

'We're pals,' she said, nodding. 'It's great to have a friend, Bob. I'm to take our share down to El Paso and wait for you there.'

'I ought not to be more than a month about it,' Oak said. 'You should be safe enough down in Texas.'

'Aren't you putting too much trust in me?' she asked.

He was, of course, all things considered; but felt

that a lot depended on his trust. 'I don't think so,' he replied easily. 'My trust about matches your responsibility. And don't fret about your brother and those other dead men. The guys from Presterville will soon send a party back to take care of all that. The burying will get done.'

She nodded sadly, kicking at her mount. 'So long, Bob.'

'Be seeing you, Sally,' he answered, watching her resume the southward course as he turned his horse into the north.

The dog was still there. It went racing on ahead of its new master, barking joyously. Oak thought of dead men and what they left behind them. He had gained a dog of one, the sister of a second, and a fortune of a third. He believed he had been blessed. But only time would tell. And that would be another story.